Turning Up the Heat

Turning Up the Heat

LAURA FLORAND

LAURA FLORAND

Chapter One

I t was incredible how much energy he had. Léa could literally no longer believe in it. The unfaltering, unfailing will that drove her husband out of bed at five, that kept him going until midnight, that sent him up to Paris to film some *Top Chef* contest when anyone else would be begging for sleep, and that kept him, the whole train ride, sketching ideas, talking to some peer who wanted his consulting skills, calling a supplier.

Léa used to watch Daniel on the train ride. To talk to him about the next job or the show, between calls. To put a finger on one of his sketches and say, *Oh, I like that.*

Then she started to read a book.

And lately, she just slept. Or didn't go up to Paris with him at all.

It was incredible how much energy he had. Because she felt like something old dropped off a cargo boat mid-storm, tossed in waves for years until it was washed up on the beach. Ready for some conscientious beach walker to pick up and toss in the trash.

Daniel had always had that drive. From the first moment she had met him, when he had taken one look at the restaurant owner's daughter and gone for her like an arrow to a target.

Her father had been indulgent. The teenage Daniel had fast become his kitchen protégé, and her father

1

loved the idea that his little girl would fall for a man just like her papa.

When her father died from an unexpected heart attack a year later, Léa had been terrified. This big three-star restaurant and all its staff, now hers. And all the critics zooming in, to strip it of its stars in her incompetent, female, eighteen-year-old hands. That's what they all said about her. Blogs and forums had been full of it: *What will happen to the Relais d'Or now?* And she had two younger siblings and had just started a ridiculously impractical arts degree, no likelihood of a real income for years. It hadn't mattered *before*. Her father was larger than life, happy to indulge his daughter in as many years as she needed, to find her artistic path in life. And then he was gone.

Just like that.

Daniel had married her almost before the will was read, and he had taken over the restaurant. *Don't worry. I've got it.*

He had been amazing. She had pulled whatever gift for publicity she could from her art skills, dragged on all her creativity, and poured it all into supporting him. She had had her own flair, it turned out. For finding television spots he could appear on. For landing articles in newspapers. For getting the mayor to reserve their restaurant when a group of actors came to town to film.

And he had climbed. Had he ever climbed. The restaurant had, indeed, lost a star two years later, when he was only twenty-one. He had known it was coming—there was no way Michelin would let a twenty-one-year-old keep a great chef's three stars. But he had fought so hard that she had bandaged more burns than anyone could ever count, in his wild will not to lose another one and to get that third one back.

He never had lost that second star, which had stunned everyone. Twenty-one! And then by the time he was twenty-seven, he had regained the third.

Léa was twenty-six when the restaurant got back that star. But where everyone talked about how young he was, how extraordinary, how driven, no one talked about her at all.

She handled accounts, and interviewing people for jobs, and firing them if Daniel didn't do it in a flash of hardness during a kitchen crisis. Things it made her sick to do at first. The firing. God, the firing was awful. She had been sick for three days, nerving herself up to the first one, and thrown up immediately afterward.

But she had done it. Eighteen years old and not even reaching the man's shoulder, standing there while he shouted at her, until Daniel realized somehow from the kitchens what was happening and came in and tore into the other man, yelling, Daniel himself only nineteen to the man's thirty, an adolescent who had to establish his authority *now*, instantly, no chance to develop it as he worked his way up.

No one had believed in them, the two teenagers. No one except them, because they had to. They had to desperately.

And the next person she had had to fire, she had done it without Daniel's help. That woman had cried. She would have to take her children out of their wonderful school, and she claimed the public one was so bad that their lives would be ruined. Léa had crawled under her desk after the woman had left and huddled shaking. She had had nightmares about those children for weeks.

But she had done it.

Because Daniel couldn't do everything, and he was working so hard, and—she loved him so much it hurt her in some deep and utter way how little she saw him. Well, she saw his profile, she saw his quick smile for her, she saw his tension and his drive. But so very, very rarely could he stand still and just—talk to her. Let her talk to him. About something other than that all-consuming restaurant and whether they should hire someone else or fire someone else or run an ad or...all those decisions that pressed down on them like concrete on grass, crushing the chance for anything else to bloom.

The accounts were just—tediously horrible, giving her a headache, filling her head with numbers until she thought of them even at dinner or walking on the beach, times when she used to think of what the light looked like on the water.

Daniel took every television spot she landed him. He did every gala for famous people she talked the mayor, and eventually senators, and then the President of France, into hosting there. He became a superstar. Wonderful, wonderful, wonderful. Exceptionally amazing.

Sometimes he would look up from finishing a plate on a TV set, and it was like he looked right through all those lights and straight at her, in the audience.

And she would remember those gray eyes, when he used to lean over her against the alley wall outside her father's restaurant, when it was still her father's. Teasing and young and intense and wanting her.

Making her feel wanted.

And it was funny she thought of that in those moments, because there was no way he saw her, sitting in the shadows, through those lights.

I'm so tired. She stared out from their terrace high up on the hills, out over the Mediterranean in the distance. *Why can't I have energy like his? What is wrong with me?*

I'm so tired.

What am I going to do?

Chapter Two

Daniel got back from Japan at three in the morning. It had been a good trip. The restaurant owner there had been eager to have Daniel's expertise at developing his menu and his theme, and the man was doing good things. As always when away consulting, Daniel had absorbed new ideas for himself everywhere—from tastes in markets to artistic elements in monastery gardens. He had bought Léa a necklace that intrigued him and couldn't wait to try its design in a subtle squiggle in the corner of a plate.

Sometimes he came back from trips revved up, ready for more, but that had been one hell of a flight, with delays and a double-whammy of jet lag since he had never really had time to recover in the other direction either. He didn't blame Léa for not picking him up at the airport at three in the morning, but he was a little jealous of her comfortable bed. A little disappointed. She used to travel with him everywhere, but lately she was...just sick of it, he guessed.

Actually, sometimes these days, she only came into the restaurant for the morning, and when he managed to make it home on the break between services in the afternoon, he found her sleeping, which made no sense to him, since she was usually sleeping when he left and sleeping when he got home. How could anyone sleep that much? Especially Léa, who used to have so much energy she could handle all the insane demands of the restaurant during the day, pick up her younger siblings from school, help them with their homework, applaud at their school events, swing by the restaurant after they went to bed to give him a kiss and a hard hug and pitch in for an hour or two if things were intense, and still have energy left to come up with some crazy scheme for him to be on television that she would share with him as soon as he got home at midnight.

He missed her awake. Thank God she still handled the restaurant business management, or he would never see her.

Recently, she had started talking about hiring a business manager, which made something inexplicable knot in his gut. She had left him so little chance with her already, and if she didn't have the bookkeeping to keep her in his vicinity...she would be entirely gone.

No more leaning over a sexy, shy, happy teenager who drove him crazy with hunger in the alley, reaching above her head to pluck a jasmine flower and tuck it into her hair, wondering if he could sneak her somewhere she would let him kiss her and kiss her and maybe...slip his hands up under her shirt, or even...

He smiled, despite his fatigue, rinsing the flight off in the guest bathroom so he wouldn't wake her. But sometimes she liked for him to wake her, sliding into bed with her late at night.

She would roll over sleepily, and he would lean over her, stroking her hair back, and her face would light into a smile before she was even properly awake. And he would kiss her, sinking gently, hungrily into her, and know that despite how much his life seemed to be consuming him, everything would be all right.

The windows were shuttered, which was unusual. They lived up in the hills, overlooking a valley of roses on one side, with a far view of the sea from another, and Léa always slept with the shutters open, and in the summer the windows themselves. She loved the sight of moonlight sparkling on the water or gilding the great fields of roses far below. She liked the sound of the cicadas and the wind.

He cast a doubtful glance into the pitch blackness of the bed, not wishing to disturb her, but finally cracked open the shutters to let in some moonlight, because the place made him feel claustrophobic otherwise. He spent enough of his life in tight spaces.

Then he turned back toward the bed—and something cold tremored through him.

The bed—didn't look right. He came closer, and this time the shock was so hard it hurt his heart. The bed was empty.

He had to shake himself, take a deep breath. Léa must be in the master bathroom, or in the kitchen getting water, or sitting on the terrace watching the full moon rise.

But she wasn't in any of those places.

His heartbeat began to race out of control. "Léa?" He started to shout, flicking on lights. Where the hell was she? "Léa?"

The house was terrifyingly empty.

His phone bleeped suddenly multiple times in his pocket, finally getting enough reception to burp up all the messages it hadn't been able to access while he was on the plane.

He yanked it out of his pocket, and relief surged through him so hard at the sight of her name, he had to grab hold of the table to steady himself. Okay. Okay. She must have gone somewhere. To a friend's for dinner, had a glass too many, and stayed the night, something like that. The Rosiers below were famous for throwing parties and filling a big upstairs room with mattresses, so that nobody had to restrain their alcohol intake or leave at a wise hour.

He kind of didn't like it, when she went without him, because—drunk people letting all their wild fun out, lots of mattresses—it wasn't that he didn't trust her, but...he hated it when she went without him. But he had never tried to stop her, because...because he knew he could trust her—he thought he knew, although, *merde*, sometimes he felt like he had barely seen her for years—and it would be cruel to limit her fun for him. Stupid and jealous and selfish.

He hit the voicemail. "*Coucou, chéri.*" Her voice sounded odd. Wistful and a little nervous. Anxiety tightened again, and he pivoted, still half-searching for signs someone had dragged her off against her will and was now holding her hostage. "I'm sorry to sneak out on you this way. You must be on the plane already. I just—needed to get away for a while." A little nervous laugh. It made him want to surge out of shadows, eviscerate the man holding a gun to her head while she made this call, a bastard who had sure as hell messed with the wrong knife skills. "I'm, ah—I know you're going to think this is crazy, but—I'm going to Tahiti. I think I'll stay a week or two. I'm not sure exactly. I'll try to call you in a few days. I just need a break. I..." She clearly had no idea what to say next. And suddenly, brightly: "I hope you had a great flight!" The voicemail ended.

Daniel pulled his phone away from his ear and stared at the moonlight over the valley of roses. What?

He hit call back immediately, no longer giving a damn if he woke her up. A cricket chirped from her bedside table. Her phone. He stared at it and actually almost started to leave a message, so intense was his need to talk to her. But then he realized how stupid he was being and slowly hung up.

"Wh—what the hell is going on, Dan?" His neighbor Grégory stumbled as Daniel dragged him out in front of his house two hours later. After listening to that message over and over. After sitting on their bed gnawing at it. After hunting through the house to see exactly what she had taken—not her family heirlooms, at least. A deep breath there. And he didn't see her wedding rings abandoned anywhere.

"Did you see anything?" Daniel gestured toward the view of his own house. "Any signs of trouble?"

"Danny...it's not even dawn yet. Wait—what? What do you mean—trouble?"

"Léa is gone."

"*What?*"

"She said she was going on a little trip," Daniel said, but then wished he hadn't. He didn't want to falsely reassure anyone who might help in the search. "I just—did you see her when she left yesterday?"

"Sure, she waved. She did have a suitcase."

"Did you see anyone in the back of the car?" Daniel asked tensely.

Grégory gaped. "You mean—like a lover? *Merde*, Dan...do you think...?"

Daniel stared at him in white shock, feeling as if the man had just detonated a grenade in his belly. "A *lover*? You think she has a *lover*?"

"No." Grégory backed up a step.

Daniel followed. "What the fuck have you seen?"

"*Nothing!* Just...when you said about someone being in the car—"

"Someone forcing her to go! Her voice sounded funny! Not a—*lover*, damn you."

"No! No. She seemed—fine. Happy, even."

That stopped Daniel for a moment. He looked back over at his house. "Happy?"

"You know. Like someone going on a vacation, in fact."

"Oh." Daniel continued to stare at his house. He couldn't remember what it was like to go on a vacation. In his teens, his father had taken him camping in the mountains sometimes. He had given all that up for Léa.

And she hadn't even *invited* him?

Not that he knew when he could have gotten away, but...

He rubbed the back of his neck. "All right. All right. Sorry."

"Were there *signs* of foul play?" Grégory asked, still worried by Daniel's worry.

"No, I—no."

"She had a suitcase. She must have packed."

"She forgot her toothbrush," Daniel said lamely. Not really a sign that a woman had been drugged and dragged out of the house, when you looked at it closely.

"You must be jetlagged out of your mind," Grégory decided finally, giving him a clap on the shoulder. "Give her a call. She probably won't mind being woken up, if you're this worried. I'm sure she's fine."

Daniel went back into his house, sat down on her side of the bed, and stared at her phone. After a minute, he picked it up, typed in her code, and started checking through all her recent calls.

"So you're still here," Daniel said flatly to Matthieu Rosier. Called by Léa at 11:23 a.m. yesterday.

Matthieu pulled his big body out from under one of the extractors and stared up at him from flat on the concrete. The whole place stank of solvent. Matt was a third cousin of Léa's, distant enough that the fact that Léa and he got along so splendidly didn't always sit well with Daniel. He was also single and went after what he wanted, and Léa was clearly gorgeous. All those angles of her cheekbones and shoulders and wrists, an athlete or a poet, the brown dust of freckles over her skin, the straight straw hair, and the way her smile bloomed out, infectious and shy and enthusiastic. Who could help wanting to please her? Daniel never had been able to.

"What?" Matt growled. "It's the middle of the rose harvest, and this *putain d'extracteur* is broken. Where do you think I'm going to be? Off in Tahiti?"

Daniel took a hard step forward. "What do you know about Tahiti?"

"Léa seems to think all her problems will be solved there, although personally, it sounds humid and boring to me. Be interesting to see how the tiare flowers grow, though." Matt wiped grease off his hands and reached for a wrench.

"*What problems?*" Daniel said between his teeth. How the fuck much better could he be for her? He never stopped. *I'll deserve this.* A very young man with his head lifted high, getting married in a fourteenth-century church, to a girl who was trusting everything she possessed to him. *I promise I'll deserve you.*

Matt looked at him, startled. "Nothing in particular. I think she just wants an adventure, a change of scenery. *Merde*, Danny, why don't you take your wife on a belated honeymoon or something? Might do the two of you good."

Daniel stared at him incredulously. "*I'm busy.*" He never, ever, ever stopped. Even the five hours he slept a night, he was usually working in his dreams. "And when have you been talking to Léa?"

"She ate lunch with us yesterday." During the rose harvest, as during the jasmine harvest, even those of the Rosier family not usually directly involved with the production of raw materials often pitched in, particularly when there were problems with the short-term labor supply. And the family, as well as some of the closer, longstanding employees, would all eat together under an old oak tree in between the extraction plant and the old patriarchal farmhouse. Léa liked sometimes to join them, boxing up macarons or some special cake from the restaurant to share, and once in a while, on a Monday when the restaurant was closed, Daniel managed to join her.

It was—really nice when he could. Sitting in the shade, talking to their neighbors, her distant cousins, sipping wine someone had thought to set aside ten years ago to bring pleasure to their later selves. It made him feel—young again. It made him turn his head in his chair and smile at Léa in a lazy, easy pleasure, and almost always, if he still had time, he would make love to her later in their room high above the sea and roses. Everything happy. Everything pleasure. Monday afternoon.

If he wasn't in Japan, or Paris, or tracking down some supply issue before it ruined the restaurant, it was his favorite time of the week.

Lately, especially as Léa grew more detached somehow from the restaurant, it often seemed as if he worked all week just for that one afternoon. Sometimes he worked all month for it, having to work through Monday after Monday but knowing that eventually, a week or two or three from now, he would manage to sink into another Monday with her again.

"What did she say?" Daniel asked.

Matt looked rather blank. "I don't know. I just remember us talking about Tahiti. Did anyone ever dream of running off there, that kind of thing."

Léa had never mentioned Tahiti to him in their entire life together. Maybe when they were teenagers, before her father died, she had said something about it being fun to honeymoon in Hawaii? Before they had seriously talked about marriage, two kids playing with the idea without ever really broaching it. He had liked the daydream himself, imagining them snorkeling among bright-colored fish and him being an instant success at surfing, striding cockily out of the waves toward Léa, stretched in a bikini under the shade of a palm tree.

But her father's death had put paid to any possibility of a honeymoon. Still to this day, when Daniel remembered that time after her father's funeral and the pressure on him at nineteen not to lose that restaurant for her by losing all its stars, the hair rose all along the back of his neck and his skull tightened.

And Léa. *Putain*, but she had been brave. Putting her trust in him. Setting her shoulder beside his. *We are in this together. And I love you.*

Merde, had she been wanting a honeymoon in the tropics all this time? Why hadn't she ever said anything?

And rising under that, something colder, deeper, darker, that he didn't know how to articulate except in hunting for kidnappers or possible adulterous lovers: when a wife disappeared for a "week or two, I don't know" without even talking about it with her husband first, what did that really mean? Had she *left* him?

Was she thinking about leaving him?

Was she deciding that right now?

Why would she leave him? *What more could he possibly do for her?*

Chapter Three

Léa lay on the wooden deck over the water on day three of her escape, head on her folded arms, gazing at the colored fish swimming in aquamarine water. The heat baked into her back. She felt like a solar panel, energy slowly charging from that sun. Recently constructed on one of the more remote and lesser-known French Polynesian islands, the resort clearly wasn't drawing the clientele hoped for. Thus the Internet deal that had caught her attention and started her thinking about running away to the tropics, the escape nearly affordable.

Not that they were hard up. Daniel's fees for consulting and *Top Chef* appearances were outrageous, and the restaurant itself did extremely well. Back when she was terrified she would manage to lose everything her father had worked for before he was even cold in his grave, she had learned how to cut pennies without affecting quality, how to run it efficiently, without waste of people or products. She and Daniel used to fight sometimes, him insisting that some food item had to be absolute top quality, her arguing against the price, until he kissed her desperately and said, *Trust me, trust me, trust me.*

So she would try to trust him. Try to relax. And he had deserved that trust and more.

The first tear drops, thinking of that, surprised her. Her eyes opened very wide, staring into the aquamarine, but another drop fell and there wasn't a cloud in the sky, only a long-tailed white bird flying toward the sun.

More tears. A silent rain of them. She didn't know where they had come from, and the orange fish bobbing up at their plop slipped away frustrated that they could not eat them.

What *was* this? She raised her hand to her cheeks, still not convinced that the tears could be coming from her. But yes...those were her cheeks that were wet.

I'm so tired. That must be it. *What the hell is wrong with me?* She had even taken a pregnancy test at one point, her stomach knotting, but it had come up negative. She had put her hands over her face, almost sick with relief and something else, an inconsistent grief. It filled her with a strange dread, to think of children. And yet she was twenty-nine and had been married more than ten years.

The dread centered all around Daniel. His gray eyes flashed in the middle of it. But he had never brought up children at all.

She closed her eyes on the tears and the disappointed fish and fell asleep.

Léa's sister raised her eyebrows to see Daniel in the doorway to her apartment and looked past him down the hall. Her eyebrows knit, and her gaze shot back to his face, searching now, worried.

"You—haven't seen Léa." It was obvious already.

Maélys's eyes widened. His sister-in-law was...what she was. Blonde like her older sister but much more glossy: polished and elegant in that edgy but vaguely academic way, always in some chunky boot heel and fitted jeans. Daniel had liked her and her brother better when they were younger, more innocent, more vulnerable, and less ensconced in the idea that Léa would take care of them. As they grew older and he and Léa supported them while they got their first degrees at the university, and then their second, because, God forbid that *they* should have to do something practical for a living, they had started to set his teeth on edge. Maélys had gotten her *maîtrise* in history, for God's sake, finishing at the age of twenty-three. When Léa, only three years older, had given up her hope of an art degree at eighteen to take care of them and never once mentioned it again.

At fifteen, Maélys had been a cute enough kid, and Daniel had taken on the responsibility of two teenagers—two teenagers even younger than Léa and himself—the same way he had taken on the responsibility for everything else. Just—done it. These days, Maélys seemed like an over-glamorized, manicured version of Léa, and the need for the real thing made his stomach knot so hard it would be a wonder if his internal organs ever let him eat again.

"Léa's *missing*?" Maélys said, on a breath of panic, which well she should feel, given that Léa was the warm hearth at which her siblings curled up. It would be so damned cold without her. He felt icy just letting the possibility ghost past his thoughts.

He fisted a hand, warring with himself. *Nobody* helped him, once they knew Léa had left a message. But... "She went on a trip," he said reluctantly. Because, *merde*, Maélys had lost her mother when she was ten and her father when she was fifteen, and her face was going very white, her eyes getting that bleak, stunned look they used to have when he would find Léa stroking her hair, looking so helpless and sad herself he didn't know what to do. Except work harder.

Maélys blinked a few times. And reached out to grab the doorjamb, taking a deep breath, that white pressure around her mouth easing. "A—trip? Léa? Who with? Hugo? I just saw him last night, and he didn't say anything about a trip."

18

"I don't think it was with Hugo." Léa taking her younger brother with her while she escaped to Tahiti was a bit of a stretch, even for her.

Maélys blinked a couple more times. "Well, then— who?" A slight edge of sulk slipped into her voice, a *why-not-me*?

"I don't know," he said tightly. "So you think it had to be with someone?"

"Well, I mean..." Maélys rubbed the nape of her neck. Her hair was up off it in an elegant deconstructed chignon. Léa usually just pulled her hair up into ponytails, unless they were going to a wedding or she was getting nervous about the fact that she had to meet the president. The time they had been invited to the Élysée, Léa had had the president wrapped around her finger in two minutes, which had been kind of fun to watch from the safety of an arm in firm possession of her waist. *Yes, she's mine. My sweetheart. I won her. You only won the fucking country.* "Why would she go away by herself?" Maélys asked. "Léa loves people."

She used to like to spend time by herself a long, long time ago, in that safe, halcyon period before her father died, when she would spend hours painting and drawing. He remembered it mostly because of the way her face would light whenever he showed up to disturb her concentration.

"Do you have anyone in mind?" he asked, his voice growing so icy that Maélys stiffened the way she had when he had had to deal with that damn predatory professor when she was seventeen. Maélys had been so hungry for a father figure. The professor had been fifteen years older than Daniel himself was, too.

"No! Daniel! I mean..." Maélys bit her lip.

Daniel's fists tightened in his pockets. "Who?"

"*Nobody*. I mean—you checked with the Rosier cousins, right?"

"*They're all here*," he said between his teeth. He felt white and sick. He should never have trusted those bastards. Third cousins. Third cousins was a relationship both too close and too far for comfort, when it involved aggressive, good-looking men Léa's age. Not that he ever had trusted them, but he had trusted *Léa*.

"And—and Marc?"

"Marc?" His *sous-chef*? What the hell? "*Marc?*"

"Well, I'm just trying to think of possibilities! You're the one who thinks she must have someone with her."

"No, you came up with that idea all by yourself," he snapped. Just like Grégory. *Putain,* how many men got a chance to lap up her smile while he was away in places like Japan? How wide a window of opportunity had he left, that everyone found it easy to assume a lover had slipped in through it? "We're very happy, Maélys."

Weren't they?

Weren't they?

"Well, of course *you* are," Maélys said very softly, with genuine, cautious pity, as if she was trying to break it to him as gently as possible. "You've got Léa."

"She's got me, too," he retorted, low and hard. *Merde*, he had worked so damn much. He was one of the top chefs *in the world*. She had something special in him, too. Damn it, she did.

"Well, she's got you some of the time," Maélys said and shook her head, half-talking to herself. "I guess it makes sense that she imprinted on Papa, but I hope to God I have more sense than to fall for a chef."

Daniel just looked at Maélys, his jaw hard. Léa's younger siblings were the most ungrateful brats. *You're welcome for making sure you were fed, clothed, and could wallow in your university studies until some little light about actually making money for yourself finally clicked in your brain. Yes, and you're welcome for making sure you didn't get pregnant by any of those men twice your age you fell for instead of a chef.*

Maélys's head tilted. She was still talking to him as if she were thinking out loud, as if whatever she said, he would be strong enough to take it. They had that conviction of his invulnerability, his siblings-in-law. His heart hiccupped in panic, as if it had looked down and discovered someone had just shoved him right up to the edge of a cliff so high he couldn't see the bottom. *Did Léa, too? Did she think he could take whatever she threw at him, too?* "Funny," Máelys murmured. "Hugo just moved out six months ago. They say a lot of couples only hold together until they can get their kids raised, and then they lose that glue and..."

Daniel reached up to grab the doorjamb over his head, digging in to hold himself up, struggling against a wave of violent sickness. The curse of his stomach. *Not that. I can't take that. Not Léa leaving me, oh, God.*

Léa. Oh, God. He got through the day just on the promise that sometime that night he would be able to *smell her hair.* Oh, shit, he could not go home to any empty bed that did not smell of her. He couldn't. He couldn't do it.

"Have you actually *seen* anything to suggest Léa might be unhappy, or are you just making all this up?" he asked tightly, fighting the nausea.

"No!" Maélys said. "But if she told you she just went on a little trip and you believe that, what are you doing here scaring me?

Chapter Four

Léa strained to get aloe gel on her back. The sunburn ached all along the outside of her triceps, her neck, and the whole of her back except the strip of skin protected by the band of her bikini. The backs of her knees stung so badly all she wanted to do was lie on her stomach, but of course, if she did that on the beach during daylight hours, they might have to fly her to a hospital. When she did sit, she balanced precariously on the part of her butt that had been covered by her bikini bottom.

But oddly, the sunburn pain seemed to wake a little energy in her.

So she rubbed a whole bottle of aloe gel on herself through the course of the day and bought a loose, white, long-sleeved cotton tunic from the resort's gift shop, which clung unpleasantly to her sticky skin. Hiding from the sun, she went for a hike through the tropical forest to a waterfall a couple of kilometers back from the coast and stood in the cold water for ages, surrounded by rich green forest and glimpses of white and red flowers.

"Do you know where I might buy paints?" she asked the young manager at the hotel reception desk, who was doing double-duty as receptionist until his resort had enough guests to justify hiring more staff.

He looked blank. Then he called to a young woman passing through the airy, rattan- and palm-filled lounge and talked to her in Tahitian. The woman shook her head, too, and they both looked at Léa worriedly.

"It's all right," she said and bought a notebook with tropical island motifs filling its page corners: tiare flowers, waves, outrigger canoes, waterfalls.

She perched on the non-burned portion of her butt in the evening on the deck outside her overwater bungalow and tried to draw the moon on the water. A frustrating exercise—moonlight with a pencil—that turned into Daniel's face and gray eyes and the Southern Cross framing it.

She hoped he wasn't missing her too much and turned the page suddenly, closing his face out of her view. That made her feel so much lighter that she was surprised when a great tear splashed on the fresh page.

What *was* wrong with her?

But it felt oddly good to cry like that, perched there watching the moonlight and the soft lagoon waves, with far out the higher waves crashing against the reef. Silent tears, with no spasms, sparkling with stars and moon.

She missed her father suddenly so much, it was as if she had never cried for him, back then. Maybe she hadn't cried enough. There had been so much to do. And Daniel had needed her. He couldn't do it alone, all that for her.

She missed Daniel so much. But she had no sense that going back would solve that problem.

And worst of all, she thought she missed herself.

But she didn't even know what self that was.

She was so tired again. She went into her bungalow, with all the windows open to the waves that lapped around it, and fell asleep.

Day Four. Léa's tunic top prickled against her sunburned skin. She wondered if she could stay here forever.

Daniel might miss her.

He might.

She sighed. She didn't know why he might, though. She must be a dead weight on him, all that energy, all that drive. He needed someone like—oh, maybe one of those elegant women who hosted him on their television shows. Someone with energy and ambition to match him.

What had happened to hers? How had she grown so ill-suited to him?

Or had he just grown so big, while she had become nothing at all?

She went for a long, long walk on the beach, all the way to the next point, stopping sometimes to draw pictures in the sand.

The effort made her feel oddly rested. The waves brought peace.

Almost back to her bungalow, she stopped at the sight of a surreal figure in that tropical world. In pants and shirt, his hands in his pockets, he stood gazing at her first sand-drawing, a rough sketch of the hills framing the Mediterranean island that could be seen from their bedroom window back home. Masculine and strong and unbreakable, black hair a little long, revealing the wave in it, a lean, beautiful body that never stopped, a steady, clean profile that filmed so well.

He looked up from the drawing to meet her eyes, and a hard breath moved through his body and sighed out of it. "Léa," he said with profound relief. But he did not run toward her. He did not walk toward her. He did not take his hands out of his pockets. He watched her warily.

His wariness built wariness in her, slowing her steps as she came closer.

"Daniel," she said, stopping the other side of the big drawing. They had been married for more than ten years. There was no problem at all between them. And yet she could not go closer.

His face grew somber. Funny how his face always held for her a trace of the teenager with the shaggy hair and the intense gray eyes who had first teased her into letting herself be kissed. As if she had never gotten to know any other him.

"You would rather I hadn't come," Daniel said quietly.

She hadn't the slightest idea. She took another step toward him. Maybe, yes. His energy made her so...empty.

The line of his pockets shifted, a gesture she knew well, his hands clenching in them. "Is there someone here with you?"

She blinked at him a moment. "A friend?" she finally guessed.

Now his jaw hardened. He looked very bleak and dangerous suddenly. "Yes."

"No. I wanted to be by myself."

"Ah." He looked down at the sand and scrubbed his toe in a small half-circle under the sketched hillside. He stared down at his foot for a long moment—he was still wearing shoes—and then without a word turned and walked back toward the bungalow.

Léa stayed on the sand, no idea what she would say or do when she followed him, no desire to enter that bungalow with him and share that space of quiet and peace. The Southern Cross was up, far away across so many miles of ocean it was like there was nothing else in the world but sea and stars.

Out of the corner of her eye, motion. Daniel had the battered duffel he favored slung over his shoulder and was heading down the wooden walkway from her bungalow.

Her heart jolted. She ran suddenly, without thought, her toes digging into the sand, splashing through water, so that she didn't have to go around to where the walkway started near the main hotel.

Daniel stopped and looked down at her. Her white tunic clung soaked to her skin, moonlight and tiki torches lighting the water around them. He didn't say anything, and he didn't reach for her to help her out of the water.

She touched her fingers to the edge of the walkway, lagoon wavelets lapping her chest-high, her face on level with his feet. "You're going?"

His jaw flexed. "You know, Léa, I might like an island vacation, too. But since you don't want to share yours and I don't have two days to spend traveling to some *other* lost-in-the-Pacific island, I'll go over there"—he pointed to a dark, empty *fare* on the far side of the lagoon, past half a dozen other little bungalows over the water—"and hope that doesn't impinge too much on your enjoyment."

He strode down the walk, his shoes loud in a world of flip-flops and bare feet. At the corner where the wooden walkway turned to join up with another bungalow's, he stopped abruptly and pivoted back. "And are you *out of your mind* to spend three hours walking on a beach by yourself at night, when no one even knows where you have gone, in something that turns transparent the first second a man tosses you into the waves? *Merde,* Léa." And he turned again and strode off.

In the stupid bungalow, over on the opposite side of the lagoon from *his wife*, Daniel threw his duffel into a corner so hard it bounced and shoved the door violently. The action reminded him oddly of shoving some guy back from Léa and out of her office, yelling, some employee who didn't want to respect an eighteen-year-old girl's authority and wasn't too happy to accept a nineteen-year-old man's either. But he had done it, furious. Those first few years, they had gotten by on nothing but desperate determination, hers to save her father's restaurant and his to be as big a man in her life as her father had been. *You're my world, I'll do everything I can to be the best thing in yours.*

What the fuck was going on?

She hadn't even *smiled* to see him on the beach. He had kind of thought—hoped, all right—that she might burst into that delighted grin of hers and run toward him.

At least she hadn't been walking back hand in hand with someone else.

Putain.

He couldn't believe the thoughts that were eating at him—about *Léa*, who would never, *never* do something like that. But...she would never run off to the South Pacific and not want to take him with her, either.

Or so he would have thought.

He sat on the edge of the bed, the moonlight gliding into the room to light a section of glass floor through which he could see the night water even while he buried his head in his hands. His stomach turned. It was the ultimate irony for someone in his profession that when he got too stressed, sometimes he couldn't eat for days.

He had to go into the kitchens and master the food again, tame it, until he and it reached some kind of rapport again where he could eat. And by mastering it, he didn't mean in those damn *Top Chef* contests which he *hated*. Media putting two top chefs through their paces like they were some damn performing monkeys and daring to judge what they came up with. But Léa had squealed so much with delight the first time he got on the show, at twenty-one, which had knocked the restaurant reservations skyward, and even more the first time he won, at twenty-three, which had booked them solid for three months. She had been dancing all around him, hugging him over and over, and kissing his face everywhere she could reach.

So he just thought of that, when he did them. Thought of her kisses raining wildly all over his face. It focused him extraordinarily. Commentators often talked about his calm during the competition, the half-smile on his face in that blaze of stress.

No kisses for freeing himself from all his obligations and showing up by surprise on her deserted island escape, though. He had had to go through her emails for the reservation confirmation and check out their credit card purchases to even find out where she had gone. *Tahiti*, it turned out, having been her very vague term for a few million square kilometers of the South Pacific.

He hung his head more deeply, his hands locked, fighting his stomach for control.

LAURA FLORAND

Chapter Five

When Léa first saw Daniel the next morning, she tripped and fell off her little deck into the aquamarine water. The fish darted away from her and she surfaced, conscious of the fact that she was in that white tunic top again, although this time her skin had healed enough to tolerate a bikini top under it.

In shorts and a T-shirt, Daniel paddled up beside her and looked down at her, his expression very neutral. Daniel, in a kayak. It was almost like catching him playing.

His arms and legs were pale—he spent so much of his time in protective kitchen gear that even the Provençal sun didn't have a big enough window of opportunity to tan him. But the body was strong and extremely controlled, of course, and even though he had never gone kayaking in the entire time they had been married, he seemed already to have the hang of it. Maybe he had been out for hours already. She had stayed awake very late and thus slept very late, but when she woke, staring at her pseudo-thatched ceiling, she had, for once, not felt the least tired.

Kind of rejuvenated. Like she wanted to go exploring somewhere. Or exploring someone. Even two someones.

"You should be careful," she told Daniel. "When you're not used to the sun..."

He shrugged. "Do you want a ride?"

She looked at the empty front seat, hesitating, and Daniel's face stiffened. "Why don't we get two one-person kayaks?" she suggested tentatively. "It's more fun."

"How do you know that?" Daniel asked tightly. "Have you ever kayaked before?"

No, but—"It sounds more fun. To be able to go where you want and not just be along for the ride."

He stared at her a long moment, his kayak barely rocking in the protected lagoon. "Fine," he said evenly. "Hop in, and I'll take us over to where they have the kayaks."

She put her hands around the edge of the kayak— and had the startled realization that she was suddenly in control here. If she flipped that kayak or held it still, there was not much he could do to resist it. "How long have you been out, and did you put on sunscreen?"

"The sun wasn't even up when I went out, and you know I hate that stuff."

He did, too. He always scrunched his face up, wincing and enduring, on the rare occasions when they spent a day at somebody's outdoor wedding and she forced him to sit still while she put it on him. His distaste had always made her laugh, given some of the things he handled as a top chef. This was a man who, in the first years in kitchens at fifteen, had been given jobs like prepping snails and intestines, as he liked to tell chef-hopefuls when he was on television shows.

She dragged the kayak to her little dock, looping one of its cords around the boat hook. "Wait a minute."

It only took her a second to come back with a beach bag and a bottle of sunscreen.

"Oh, *putain*," Daniel muttered when he saw it.

She laughed, a sparkle of energy and happiness that surprised her.

Daniel laid his paddle across the kayak, his eyes caught on her face. "You're not mad at me for something, then?" he asked softly.

She shook her head, her laughter fading. "I just wanted to get away for a little bit. I thought if I tried to ask you, you would be too busy until five years from now, and the impulse would fade, and I would never manage to do it." That was partly true, but not entirely true. When she really thought about having him with her—she hadn't wanted to risk it. She had gone the day before he got back, on impulse, just in case he might have tried to come with her.

He nodded and looked out to sea, squinting his eyes against the reflection on the water.

"Here." She gestured with the sunscreen.

He didn't even make a face this time, as he swung out of the kayak onto the dock, lost in thought. But when she started to apply the sunscreen to his arms, he pulled off his T-shirt. "Might as well get the whole thing."

He sat on the edge of the dock with his feet in the water, facing out to sea, while she squirted handfuls of sunscreen into her palms and began from his back, rubbing over his shoulders. He had spent all his life in a profession that demanded speed, strength, grace, agility, and all of that without pause, unrelentingly. While there were chefs who managed to put on weight despite this, from their sheer love of food, Daniel was only thirty, and anyway, there were days he would not eat at all and get pissed off at her when she tried to push him. So he had a beautiful body. All lean strength, no fat.

It was nice. Nice to be able just to stroke those shoulders, to appreciate the smooth skin and the strength underneath it. It had always fascinated her, the way his chest and jaw could prickle but his back be like a baby's skin.

She sank into the feel of it, smiling a little.

"It wasn't—that stupid announcer who kept trying to flirt with me on that last show?" Daniel asked suddenly, still staring out to sea. "I handled that right, didn't I? I think she was just playing to the viewers."

"Aurélie Rochelle? She's just having fun. Isn't she almost twice your age?" With a shrewd, wry wit and warmth which pulled Daniel's own warmth and humor out of him. The two of them always had a good time, when Daniel was on her show. Léa wasn't sexually jealous of Aurélie, but she was jealous, just the same.

"No, last week."

A tiny silence as Léa winced away from her admission: "I—may have missed that show."

His feet stilled in the water. He twisted to look at her. "You didn't watch it?"

"I—" A lot of times these days, she didn't watch his shows. They had started making her feel so— hopeless. Once she had caught herself crying in the middle of one, for no reason she could explain, and decided it must be that time of the month. "I think I was helping my sister get moved into her new apartment. I forgot to record it."

"They put the link up on the web."

As shows pretty much always did. "Ah."

The muscles under her hands tightened, until she thought he might suddenly shove himself off the dock into the water. But he stayed. Bending his head as she stroked that sunscreen into him.

He really had the most beautiful body. Funny, now when she looked back at their wedding pictures, she could see how young he had been. How he had filled out, filled into himself, becoming more strongly masculine as he grew older. But even as a half-formed teenager, he had always seemed hot to her. Sexy and perfect and he could just zero in on a girl, with that little teasing smile.

Make her feel the most wanted, the most wonderful, the most precious thing in his whole world.

She slid the cream down his arms. It seemed like her whole life she had loved his arms. How strong they were, how they could hold her, how they could reach high up things for her. Like stars.

Things she couldn't get herself.

She frowned, circling the cream slowly into the backs of his hands.

"Did the doctor have—news?" he asked suddenly, sounding stifled.

"What?" What doctor?

"Wasn't that why you couldn't go up to Paris with me, a doctor's appointment?"

It had been a legitimate excuse that time. And...she hadn't traveled with him since. "That was three months ago!"

"Oh." His eyes flicked over her stomach, and he turned his head sharply away. "So—no news."

"I'm not pregnant," she said quietly. He flinched a little, but she had no idea whether it was in disappointment or relief. Good God, kids. The thought of finding herself a mother, now, made her feel as if she was being buried under something and slowly crushed. "I just wanted a vacation. I guess you can't understand that," she added ruefully.

He cut her a sharp, incredulous glance. "Not understand wanting a *vacation*?"

"You can understand it?" she asked blankly.

"*Putain*, Léa. What do you think I'm made of?"

Stardust, probably. Something hard and brilliant, born out of the fires of the universe. With gorgeous gray eyes.

"I would have wanted mine with you, though," he said low, ground out, gripping the dock and staring at the water around his toes.

Oh. Léa sat on the edge of the dock beside him. She didn't know what to say. Except that he had the most beautiful back in the world and she could have stroked cream into it forever, but maybe that wouldn't add to the conversation.

Daniel took a slow breath, and she looked up from that hard grip of his beautiful, strong hand to find him watching her sideways, an elusive gleam of gray through those thick black lashes of his.

"You didn't do my chest." He picked up her hand to squirt sunscreen in it. "It's my least favorite part."

He twisted to sit cross-legged facing her, pressing her palmful of sunscreen against his right pectoral. It was true that it was his least favorite part. He hated the way it smeared in his chest hair. He had several times, in fact, threatened to shave his chest if she insisted on the sunscreen, but always yielded.

She knelt in front of him, watching her hands knead the cream into his muscles. She loved his chest, too. Liked the feel of it, when she curled up against it, liked the taste of it, liked to rub her face back and forth against all his textures when they made love...

She got lost in the pleasure of kneading cream into his chest, her hands running over and over him, until a hand curled into her hair, and he kissed her, a long, slow, deep hello of a kiss, like he kissed her sometimes at one in the morning, sliding into bed beside her. Like he kissed her sometimes on those rare Monday afternoons that were like sunlit, precious daydreams scattered through her life.

Her mouth warmed to him instantly, as if he was some heady ambrosia she could drink to make her glowing.

He made a hungry sound, his other hand coming up to join the first, angling the kiss as he dragged her into his lap. "Léa," he muttered into her mouth. "Léa. I missed you."

Really? There were moments in his life when he had room to notice she was gone for a few days?

"Ow," she whimpered softly, still angling for more of his mouth despite the pain. "Daniel. That hurts."

Startled, he loosened the hand still in her hair first, his mouth lifting. But that just brought more pressure from the hand on her back. She made a tiny sound of distress, part hunger for more of him, part sting at the contact.

Both hands flew away from her. "What did I do?"

"I'm sunburned," she said, hating to stop him and at the same time inexplicably relieved. If they made love, surely he would assume he should move into that bungalow with her, at the very least. Why did that make her feel as if nothing would ever be possible again?

He peeled the tunic off her body enough to peek down her back and grimaced. "*Chérie.*"

"And *that* was with sunscreen," she told him. "So—" She slid her hands down his ribs to get the last bit of taut stomach that tightened still more under her hands, and he drew a breath, gazing at her. Hands held wide. So very clearly wanting to touch her and not able to.

Trapped by his own respect for her pain.

She came up onto her knees again and kissed him for that, because he was so entirely wonderful. He made a little sound, responding hungrily, and she stayed on her knees a long time, kissing him more and more. There was something so—thirsty about the position. About his inability to touch her, so that she could lean into him and drink until she couldn't drink another drop...and yet still want more. She kissed him and kissed him and kissed him, in unassuageable thirst.

"*Ma chérie. Minette. Léa.*" He got lost in the kissing, too, whispering her name in ragged breaths, a flush mantling his cheekbones when she at last raised her head. His hands had dropped and dug hard into his own thighs.

He looked inexplicably, intensely—relieved. "So you're still—so that's still okay," he breathed and leaned forward, hands gripping his legs, to grab another kiss. And then another. And one more. He seemed insatiable, as if he had never kissed her before and didn't know if he would ever have a chance again.

She gave her mouth to him again and again. Yes, he still made her hungry. Even she hadn't gotten that tired.

The kissing and kissing and wanting more but not taking it reminded her with a strange sweetness of when they were teenagers. When they would kiss and make out in some secret corner, always hungry for more than they dared do. "I love you," Daniel whispered, as he would sometimes then, that little cry of kiss-maddened longing.

The three words that always made her whimper in hunger and try to bury herself deeper in him.

At last, she pulled back, feeling as if the sunburn had spread to her entire body, hot and prickly and in need of healing.

Daniel was breathing long and deep, his eyes eating up her face, something brilliant in the gray. "All right, then," he said very softly, lifting a hand to curve around her cheek. "That's good to know."

And he plunged straight into the shoulder-high water, sinking into it, the slightly overlong cut that had become part of his image floating like fine seaweed against his skull, his eyes turned up to hers even through the seawater. She had to reach down a hand to him, because he looked so much as if he was drowning.

Chapter Six

Kayaking with Daniel was fun, more fun than Léa could possibly have imagined, since she could never have imagined this. Each in a kayak, they could race, splashing and bumping each other, at first by accident, as Léa got the hang of it, and then on purpose. They could wait for each other and point at something, or one or the other of them could drive ahead. The pain of it was constant—the pressure of the low plastic seat on her sunburned back and on the backs of her legs, sweat adding its sting. But Léa never mentioned it.

They finally stopped at a little beach by a rocky outcrop that had drawn them because every third or fourth wave water blew out of a hole in it, so that from a distance they had been half-convinced it was a whale.

"If we hike back along this stream, we should find a waterfall," Daniel said. "According to the man renting the kayaks."

"Let's eat first." Léa pulled out the bag from the hotel.

Lots of tropical fruit, freshly picked and freshly cut for them, and cold pork that had been pulled to shreds. Daniel lounged on his side to eat. She sat up, to avoid too much contact between her sunburn and the grating sand, and smiled, watching Daniel taste the food, the way he sank into the flavors and thought about them, about what they did for him and what he would do differently to them.

He looked up to find her watching him and smiled back, offering her a sliver of mango from his fingers straight to her lips. It sank slow and sweet into her body, and he sucked the juice of it off his thumb as he watched her swallow.

Heat spread through her, uneasily.

"You're so pretty," he murmured, and the heat grew stronger, tickling her away from something important. It was so impossible to resist it, and yet if she lost herself to it...what chance might she lose? What was she *afraid* to lose, when they had made love so many times before?

He drew a finger gently down the back of her hand and then looked back to sea, his expression for a moment softened, as they ate.

As she ate. After the first few mouthfuls, Daniel mostly contented himself with feeding her. She took some mango and fed him back, and he liked that very much, his smile curving against her thumb and his lips catching her fingers to suck the juice off.

But he stopped bringing anything to his own mouth.

"You don't like it?" she asked at last. Daniel was, God knew, fussy about his food. She had grown up in her father's kitchens and knew how to cook quite well, even if she would never be a superstar, but so many times he had just picked at what she made him, leaving almost everything on his plate. It hurt her feelings, especially when she would take him out after one of his *Top Chef* victories to an up-and-coming bistrot and he would eat like a starving man. He infinitely preferred the latest bistrot over other starred restaurants, where he was always on the alert, like a general in a war zone, analyzing everything. And, fine, maybe the latest bistrot's food was better than hers, but...*her* food *cared*. She had kept cooking for years, in the face of his rejection, because she could still remember her mother's homey meals and how much her father had liked them, and because she had to feed her two younger siblings and she didn't want to *always* take them to the restaurant. But now that those siblings had moved out, she rarely bothered.

He gave her an incredulous look. "The fruit? If only I could get fruit this fresh in the Relais. It makes you realize you spend your whole life trying to bring people something that catches just the faintest hint of this—lying on a beach with a beautiful woman feeding you mango. I guess chefs have to offer all that elegant food to try to make up for the fact that we're damn well not going to give away the beautiful woman."

She flushed a little, looking down and then looking up again. She wasn't beautiful. She was perfectly fine, she didn't have any qualms about herself. But she was angular and freckle-dusted brown, and her straight, straw-colored hair tended to get all dry at the ends before she remembered to take care of it. Compared to those elegant television women, she was a gawky, overeager student, a good eight years too old to be one. But Daniel was clearly looking at her, when he said the word.

He sat up, and she felt him watching her under those black lashes of his in that way that had always turned her heart over. At seventeen, she had drawn and painted just his face in secret, over and over, trying to catch that look under those eyelashes and what it did to her heart.

"Léa. Did you—get bad news, from the doctor?"

It took her a second to realize he was back on that routine check-up months ago. His time just flew, didn't it? Months gone by in a minute.

"That...you couldn't have a baby? Something like that?"

She stared at him. "*No!*"

"Oh." One of his arms was looped lazily around his bent knee, in a pose she couldn't remember seeing since their escapes into the hills as teenagers. When he would lean over her in the grass and kiss her and kiss her, and they would go too far, but try not to go *too* far, and he would finally roll away, breathing hard, and stare out at the sea far away.

Now he gazed at the thumb and finger of that casually draped hand. They rubbed together, over and over. "Or...or something really bad...something like—" His face and voice tightened. "Ca-ca...something bad. That you haven't told me."

"*No!*" Léa said again, and he drew a hard gasp of relief. "Daniel. I just—I really just wanted to do something crazy. Escape to a tropical island. Haven't you ever dreamed of doing something like that?"

That hard working of his jaw. His thumb and forefinger pinched together until she saw the knuckles whiten. "I didn't dream of doing it alone," he said in that same low, ground voice in which he had said something similar, earlier on her deck.

She looked away, not knowing what to say. And realized on a breath of surprise that she didn't feel tired. Just profoundly wary of something she didn't even know how to name. "Would you have minded? If I had been pregnant? Or not able to get pregnant?"

His head whipped toward her, gray eyes wide and brilliant with shock. He sat up all the way. "Do you want us to have kids, Léa?"

Married more than ten years. And they had never once even discussed it before. "Do *you*?" she said. *No. No kids. Please no.* The thought of them made her feel like a plastic bag dropped in the middle of the *autoroute*.

Something strange and intense happened to his face. "I would have to cut back," he said flatly, as if she had been arguing with him. He twisted suddenly so that she could only catch part of his profile, his arms gripping his knees. "I won't miss most of my child's life, too," he said, low and viciously. "I *won't*."

The tone cut through her even more than the words. As if he was fighting her. She scooted on her knees to get a better view of his face. "*What?*"

"The damn *Top Chef* thing, for example. *Putain*, Léa, I'm famous enough. We don't need the money. Can't we let that go?"

If he had held her out over a cliff, opened his hands, and waved bye-bye, she would have been less shocked. She gaped at him, feeling air sail past her on the fall. "*What?*"

"Something has to go if we have kids, Léa," he said flatly. "I mean it."

She was speechless. Sliding closer to him, she slipped her hand under the hard lock his arms had around himself and rested her hand on his knee. "You don't like doing *Top Chef?*" she asked at last, blankly.

"*Putain*, Léa. Maybe the first few times, when it was my chance to prove myself to the world, to beat all the people who didn't believe I could."

She was utterly flabbergasted. She had always thought it was part of his relentless drive, the way he never said no when *Top Chef* called to ask him for another match. He *had* to beat every challenge thrown out to him, he *had* to show he was the best. "I thought you loved that."

He turned his head at last and looked at her, his eyes oddly hard, as if he was facing an enemy. "Did you?"

She stared at him. "But—you always have so much grace in there. That little smile on your face. The commentators always talk about it, how much you thrive on it."

He gazed at her for a long moment, so long she thought he might actually ask her why she was getting her information about him from television announcers. Given that they had been married for over ten years. But his mouth curved, not too differently from the way it curved when he was on *Top Chef*, when his hands were flying, his brain fermenting with brilliance as he strove to beat the opposing chef at whatever insane challenge the show threw at them, all while his mouth stayed almost tender in its calm. *He makes love to the food,* the announcers would say, *watch him.* "Do you remember the first time you got me a spot on that show? How happy you were?"

Well—yes. It had been such a coup. She had hugged him and hugged him, so happy with herself to have given him this window to shine. To show the whole world how wonderful he was.

"And do you remember the first time I won?" He stroked his own cheek, as if he was feeling something there. "You couldn't stop touching me."

She smiled. "Yes." How they had celebrated. He had been so *awesome. Absolument merveilleux.* For weeks afterward, some vision of him at a particular moment in the intense battle would flash before her eyes, and if he was anywhere within reach, she would fling her arms around him and kiss him again, just for being so wonderful. Oh, had he ever shown the world.

He looked away again. "I thrived on that."

The meaning was so strange, it had to percolate through her slowly. Like another language, with no Rosetta Stone that could help her pick it apart and make sense of it. "Wait...you didn't do it for yourself?"

A sharp gray glance. "You must not understand me. Of course I did it for myself." He touched his cheek again.

"Ah." She relaxed. That was, in fact, what she had always known. He had that drive. He wanted to be the best. She had poured everything of herself into supporting his need to be incredible.

Everything.

Something prickled through her at the thought, an almost-awareness, an answer. Was that what—

"To make you that happy with me? What man wouldn't do everything, for that?"

She was so dumbfounded, she thought she might cry. The perspective was so radically different from anything she had ever believed. He did it...he did *all that* because she kissed him?

"Léa." That inexplicable hostility had faded. Daniel touched her cheek. "Don't."

And she realized she *was* crying. Again. "*O purée,*" she muttered indignantly, making him smile a little. Probably the only reason her language stayed so clean after a lifetime in the restaurant business was the way he smiled at her polite little swear words. "Not again."

"Again?" He rubbed one tear away with a callused thumb that made her hungry for more caresses. Her face curved into his palm before any doubt could override the instinct.

She shrugged, deeply reluctant to admit to him how weak she felt right now.

"Léa." Daniel rolled back, using her wrists to tug her astride him. He had almost no control of her body with her wrists alone, so she had to cooperate, but she had never resisted Daniel. Their teenage fear of crossing lines, of going too far, and Daniel's romantic urge to treat her like something precious had been all that slowed them down.

She smiled at him a little tremulously as she settled astride him. But the warmth of his body between her thighs felt utterly perfect, pushing back that wariness she couldn't explain. Still without a shirt, he lay on the sand beneath her, all flat stomach and defined ribs and lean muscled strength. He made her want to cry again, he was so utterly beautiful.

Still loosely clasping her wrists, his thumbs stretched high to stroke down the sensitive insides of her forearms. Over and over. A caress that took over her will, melting her to him. "Léa." His voice deepened. His eyes had gone brilliant again, but nothing hard or angry in them now. He brought her hands to his mouth and kissed the palms. "I love you."

She nodded rapidly, *me, too,* feeling shaky and shivery with hunger and vulnerability and that caution that had driven her to the other side of the world without him.

He kissed up to the insides of her wrists. "Still love me, Léa?" he whispered.

Her eyes widened. "Of *course!*" How could anyone not?

He stroked her fingertips over his cheeks, petting himself with her, his eyes half closing. "So that's all right," he murmured, caressing his cheek into his own strokes.

"I told you it's nothing to do with you!"

His mouth hardened, under her palm. "Don't feel you have to repeat yourself. You've given me plenty of opportunities to grasp the point, if I choose to." He tugged her hands a little to pull her down closer to him, pressing them to the sand on either side of his head. Her pelvis rocked forward on his. Her face came close enough to his that it would be less effort to kiss him than to hold herself up. Even less effort to curl up against his chest and just stay there. He loosed her hair from its ponytail, combing it forward to brush his face. "There," he whispered with satisfaction.

She drew a long breath. The feel of his sex hardening against hers liquefied her. She could feel her eyes drifting closed, her body growing pliant and helpless. She had never been any good at this position. Arousal melted her muscles, left her too yielding and soft to take control. This position was always for playing, until his body was all one hard need to drive into her, to take her over. Until her body was all one supple need to be taken.

His hands pulled her long tunic up until he could slip under it, his fingers tracing ever so delicately the line of her bikini bottom. And then teasing over her bikini-clad butt. "I suppose this is the only space of skin where you aren't sunburned?" he whispered.

Her hips twisted against his. She nodded, already growing heavy, wanting.

His fingers followed over the little line of the string bikini. "There's not even enough space to fit my hands to grasp your hips," he murmured, twisting up suddenly with his own hips, trying to obtain pressure without gripping her.

She responded, pressing down because she knew it was what he wanted her to do, but she was shivering and losing strength. She wanted him to grab her now, drag her sex against his, take over her body. But he was bound more strongly than if he had been tied to a bedpost. He couldn't take her without hurting her.

He thrust up again with his hips, and his fingers trailed around to tuck into the front of her bikini.

She shivered again, her sex melting. His eyes glittered like stars as he watched her face, sinking his fingers lower inside her bikini.

She made a little moaning sound, her head hanging heavily. He lifted his own head off the sand enough to catch her mouth, kissing her like sex, lushly, invasive. His fingertips slipped far enough down to brush her clitoris.

She gave a little gasp and collapsed on top of him, clinging, her cheek rubbing against him like an animal. His hand got crushed between them, no wiggle room. She moaned a little, rocking her hips against his crushed fingers.

"*Chérie*, you have to sit up just a little," he whispered. "I can't turn you over, on the sand or on me. Not with your back like that. *Allez, bébé.*" He pushed her up a little by one shoulder. She tried, but when his freed fingers flicked again, deftly, all her weight sank back down, hanging against the brace of his hand.

"I want to hold you," he breathed. "I want to suck your pretty *tétons* until you babble my name. But I'll forget—I'll grab you too hard, and I'll hurt you. And you'll let me." His hand dove lushly into her parted sex. She whimpered, twisting frantically, unable to stand this position held off him. She never had been able to hold herself separate from him when she came. And yet the pleasure built in her, to be held apart and yet so helpless to him. To be so vulnerable to his deft control.

"Sit up." He pushed at her shoulder. "*Bébé*, let me do this."

"No." She shook her head, because she *couldn't*. Emotionally too shy to hold herself so exposed to him while she came, and it was a pure physical impossibility. Her muscles just didn't work that way, when his hand was in her sex.

"*Yes*," he said fiercely, his fingers thrusting into her while she shook and arched, his other hand flat on her breastbone now, forcing her off him enough to give him room.

"No, no, *no*, Daniel," she said, "*no*—" And then she was coming, convulsive little frantic waves, clutching at his hand in her, and he kept moving it, pleasure swamping her, the waves building and building and crashing again until she fell on him, kissing him wildly, and then convulsed again in one sharp, high cry and rolled away into the sand.

The sand scraped against her sunburn. After a moment, he reached and gently rolled her over onto her tummy. She buried her face in her arms.

"I like it," he whispered, fingers tracing over her skull. He blew over her shoulder, and sand skittered off her. "I like seeing you come. Don't be embarrassed."

She kept her face buried in her arms, not answering. She was very conscious of how aroused he must be, and her own body still shivered with hunger for him to drive into her. The sunburn wouldn't hurt that much, she wouldn't care...and from this position, he wouldn't have to touch *too* much sunburn. She arched her butt up just a little, shifting it back and forth in a hint.

He came to his feet suddenly. She twisted her head on her arms enough to see him stride waist deep in the waves and stand there with his hands locked in fists behind his head, staring out at the horizon.

She thought about following him, slipping in behind him and slipping her hand around to the arousal against which he was pitting the force of waves too warm to kill it.

He still stood there, and then suddenly, she didn't know why she *shouldn't* follow him, and she rolled to her knees.

But he turned at that moment and came back out of the water, still enough aroused under his suit that at first she thought he was coming back to her and she sat back on her heels. But he just gave her a little smile that made her blush crimson, and that made his smile deepen as he ducked his head and crouched down by their picnic basket, packing it with deft, fast fingers into a much better arrangement than the resort kitchen staff had ever thought of. "Let's go find that waterfall."

Chapter Seven

They hiked along the stream, a narrow, haphazard footpath that not enough feet had worn, the forest rich and thick around them, birds calling, a tree dripping flowers. Green surrounded them, and rich dark earth, and the stream flowing over dark rocks, leftover from volcanoes lost in the depths of time.

They could hear the waterfall before they reached it, but still Léa drew a breath of surprised pleasure when they came out beneath it. The stream was small, and the rocks angling above them spread it out fine, so that it fell into the pool below in a wide veil, nearly transparent. The place was a deep, magical secret, compared to the vast possibilities of the ocean. A spill of red hibiscus near the falls brightened the dark, safe colors of rock and water and green, and the waterfall shimmered with white.

She had hiked to a waterfall the day before, narrower, higher, more pounding, but also beautiful. And it was a sharp, sweet realization, how much more pleasure there was in the moment because Daniel was with her.

Already waded halfway out to the falls, she turned enough to smile at him, an absurdly shy smile for how long they had been married. But she felt shy. She felt as if she had come out here to find a piece of herself, and he already wanted that piece for himself, and she didn't even know what it looked like yet much less whether she wanted to give it away.

And she still felt embarrassed, from earlier on the beach. Soft and sticky and vulnerable.

His eyes searched hers rather gravely for a moment, and she dipped her head. His eyes narrowed at the evasion, that way she knew, that meant that nothing was going to stop him reaching what he wanted.

She shifted away from that look, feeling even more vulnerable than before—like she had a chance in hell of protecting that fragile nascence that had brought her to this island alone—and stepped under the waterfall, to wash off her sticky embarrassment over the beach.

The veil of it was a gentle pleasure to stand under rather than a pounding force. She kept her back to him, stretching up her arms to savor the sensation of the water washing over her.

Her string-tied bikini top loosened suddenly and washed entirely away. *Oh.* Her head tilted back sharply to hit a strong shoulder just as hands cupped her breasts, warm hands, and everywhere else the wash of cool water.

"Léa," he whispered, squeezing her gently, thumbing the nipples.

Oh. The pleasure of it washed through her, sweet and intense. But *oh, not again.* He was taking over every part of her.

Oh. His fingers handled her breasts so expertly, all that lovely, lovely expertise in her. She swayed back against him, washed by the water.

His hands trailed all the way down her belly as his body dropped away, her support gone. Hands gripped just the unburned front side of her thighs and turned her.

She looked down, the water parting over the nape of her neck, to find him kneeling in the water, looking up at her. His black hair was soaked and dripping, but the waterfall parted around her body, partially shielding him.

"Keep your hands up," he whispered, and she realized her hands were still where they had been when he first touched her, cupped high above her head, wrists touching, water filling them and then spilling over all around her.

She shivered all over, shaking her head, and started to lower them.

"Léa," he said.

And her breasts tightened unbearably, her sex melting. She brought her wrists slowly back together again, above her head. That made the weeping of her sex worse, her body already yielded.

"I'd tie you like that if I could," he told her, guttural. "So you couldn't turn away from me. So you couldn't tell me no." His hands, gripping the front of her thighs, wedged them apart.

"Oh, God, no, Daniel," she gasped, as his mouth met her sex, and her whole body arched into the waterfall. "*Daniel.*"

"Don't tell me that," he said fiercely. "Say *yes, I love it, I love you.*" His mouth took her in a hard, hungry fuck, ravaging her, like some starving man at last before food.

"Daniel." Her hands tangled in his hair, her body lost under the waterfall. "Don't, don't—" She arched back, shaking uncontrollably, losing words as he mastered her pleasure so easily, so expertly, building her and building her, knowing exactly what to do to her. She drew a little terrified breath, drowning in him, and then waves on waves of delight, of utter lost hunger, overwhelmed her as she came, the waterfall streaming into her face, but the pleasure stronger even than it. She couldn't come down from it, because he wouldn't let her. Keeping her lost in that pleasure until it became almost pain, and water spilled into her face and choked her. He pulled her free of the falls then, soothing her, massaging the unburned part of her thighs as he lifted his mouth from her. She was still rippling with the pleasure, shaking in little spasms that made her cling to him, as he gently, gently lowered her down into the water, holding her head above it, hand still caressing her.

Her eyes flew open again, and she stared straight into his brilliant, starved face. "You *get up*," she said fiercely, slapping her hand on his chest.

His eyes widened. "Lé—"

"You *do* what I *tell* you." She shoved at him, trying to force his much greater weight up.

"Léa." He let himself be forced to his feet, reluctantly.

She pushed him back under the waterfall, her whole body incandescent with some kind of rage or need.

"Léa," he said warily, as the water cascaded over him.

She yanked his swim shorts off.

He grabbed for them, too late. "Léa, no."

"Hold your arms out," she said fiercely. "Don't you touch me. You take it."

"Oh, *putain.*" Slowly, his body taut, he held his arms out under the water. He was already violently aroused, frustrated multiple times that day. Her hand curled around him. "*Léa. Merde*, don't—"

"Shut up." She looked at him, naked under that waterfall, arms out, body so hard, water spilling all around him like an aurora. And then she sucked him into her mouth.

Eleven years of marriage, and she had never done this. She had played a little around the idea, sometimes, kissing down his belly, hand around him. But making love always left her so overwhelmed with pleasure, and Daniel loved to take charge as she lost herself in him; it satisfied some glittering, hungry need in him. She knew all kinds of little things he liked, when he was close to coming, ways to arch her hips or squeeze her muscles or slide her hand to make him shatter with pleasure. But she had never taken him over. Made *him* come when *she* wanted.

It was harder than she thought, to fit him in her mouth. She retreated from the first effort, her hand coming up to curl around the base of his erection and then curve firmly over his testicles, a touch she knew made him moan. It made him tense sharply now, his head going back so that the water spilled straight into that honed, gorgeous face of his. Exactly as it had into hers.

She tried her tongue, touching it gently to the tip of him, and his fists spasmed so hard she felt it down the length of him. She brought her second hand into play and tried again with her mouth, circling her tongue around his tip, sliding herself over him, trying to create a little suction. Maybe her mouth was too small. How did people do this?

"*Putain. Léa.*" His hands came down to curve around her head.

She pulled her mouth away, and he made an involuntary sound of protest. "Don't you *touch* me," she told him fiercely.

"*I can't help it,*" he ground out.

"*Try harder.*"

He stared down at her, his face very flushed, the water pouring over that hard, desperate body. "Léa. Don't do this." But he didn't move away. He didn't dive into the water out of her reach.

"Shut up," she told him again. "And put your hands out."

Slowly, very slowly, he managed to pull his hands away from her head and stretch them away from his body again. Not for the first time, she wondered how she had landed such a beautiful man—and then she remembered, the restaurant. Her father's daughter. And *she* flushed, to have beautiful perfect Daniel see her like this, kneeling at his feet, clumsily trying to suck him off. She closed her eyes, so that all she could see and think about was the water sliding over his skin, and off him onto her.

Eyes shut, she felt her way back over him, with a tentative suckle. He groaned. "Léa, please don—"

She squeezed his testicles just the way he liked it, and he shut up. The water lapped all around her where she knelt, cool against her flushed body. It streamed off him and, because she was so close, slipped from him onto her, washing her in the liquid off his body. Eyes closed, she sank into the sensation of the water, so gentle, and his hardness, so very hard. She let herself get lost in the pleasure of this, like she got lost when he made love to her, no other thought. Nothing but this. All his textures and strengths and what her mouth could do. One hand curling around his testicles, she rubbed him slowly, enjoying the textures of him there, like nowhere else on his body. The hardness of his penis in her other hand. The way she could grip him, just as strongly as she liked, and he would only moan and jerk. The way she could loosen her grip, caress, and he would hiss with protest and try to shut himself up.

The way her mouth could slide over him...sink deeper...why yes, he would fit. He would fit so very well. Too hard, too big, too much, and she liked it.

Shh, her hand caressed over his testicles. *Behave*, her fingers told the base of his penis, as she reduced him to incoherent panicked begging. *You'll do what I tell you. And I like you like this.*

But he cheated. His hands shot down and fisted into her hair with one frantic cry as he came.

Afterwards, he ducked into the waterfall immediately and then behind it, sinking down into the slim sliver of tormented water between the cascade and the rocks.

Léa floated, feeling dreamy and sleepy and curiously pleased with herself, smiling at the way he hid himself.

It had taken her years to realize Daniel was profoundly shy. They must have been near their mid-twenties before it hit her. Before she realized that when he kept his arm around her waist at baptisms and weddings, quiet, letting her do most of the chatting, there were more elements involved than romantic affection. Yes, baptisms and weddings were some of their excuses to relax with each other, and maybe he didn't want to spend any more time on the other side of the *salle de reception* from her than she did from him. But where she would be at ease if they got separated, still laughing and having fun even if she would miss the touch of his hand, he would not be. It was counter-intuitive to understand this: the man who could take over a three-star restaurant and its rebellious kitchen staff at nineteen; the man who could go on TV shows and handle flirting announcers with a quiet, confident warmth; the man who could walk into a kitchen in a strange country on the other side of the world and take charge in just the right way, both confident of his own authority and respectful of the other chef. Shy. How could a man who did all that, so well, be shy?

But if he didn't know what he wanted, and he didn't know what people wanted from him, he didn't know what to do with himself or even if they wanted him around. And it had taken her seven years—six of them married—to realize this because, from the first minute he saw her, Daniel had always known what he wanted.

He had wanted his chef's daughter.

Wanted her body and her heritage and her heart. Wanted her restaurant. Wanted to take that restaurant back to the stars. Wanted to be famous, to be begged for, to be the best, to be the very best.

He had wanted it all. He had wanted so damn much. His wanting took over his own shyness, stronger than it. It was only in those rare windows of sociability, when he had no goal and others had no goal for him, that it could peek out. That his own wife could slowly realize that he wasn't bored or lost in thoughts about the kitchens while she laughed with her cousins. He had what he wanted from that situation—his hand around her waist—and he was left rudderless, profoundly uncertain of what anyone could want from him or see in him besides his work.

Well, I wanted that, she thought at him in defiant firmness, through the veil of the waterfall, and then rolled over to cool her flaming face in the pool beneath the falls.

Because she wasn't shy with her cousins. They had played together all their lives. She wasn't shy when it came to talking to other people. She knew what they wanted from her—they just wanted to laugh and joke, be happy and share their lives and have her be happy for them. But she had always felt a deep streak of shyness with Daniel, the blushing, delicate knowledge that she was so eagerly holding out her whole heart.

To serve someone else's life.

Chapter Eight

They kayaked back slowly, Léa resting her paddle frequently, her shoulders aching more and more from the unaccustomed motion, aggravated by the fact that she didn't want to lean back in her seat, the friction against her sunburned skin even harder to stand now that she was tired. Daniel's shoulders showed no signs of tiring, but then, there weren't really any muscles in his shoulders or arms or back or core that hadn't been in constant use, in all kinds of motions, since he was fifteen years old. Half his life.

"I might be able to tow you." Daniel eyed the ropes dangling at each end of the kayaks, provided to hook them to the bungalow docks. "Let's see if we can attach the cords."

"No, I'm fine," Léa said. She didn't want to be towed. Like she hadn't wanted to sit in the front seat, being taken wherever he chose. She would rather have her shoulders burn. "You can go on, if you want. I'll get back eventually."

He shot her a look, his eyes suddenly hard again, incredulous, his face tightening. "Thank you, Léa, no. I don't believe I will go off and leave my wife in a kayak by herself in the ocean, when she's overtired and having a hard time making it back. We'll have to try that some other romantic vacation." And he drove his own paddle into the water, outpacing her for some fifty meters before he turned and paddled smoothly back to her. His face was calm but set again, and for the rest of the trip back, he looked more out over the ocean than at her.

The sun was setting when they reached her dock, a beautiful wash of orange-pink across the water, a hush falling over the sea. He hooked both their kayaks to her dock and leaped up first to help her out of hers. He didn't let go of her hands once she was stable, looking down at them, playing with her wedding rings. He didn't wear a ring. His hands had grown bigger, since the age of nineteen, and it didn't make sense to get him another one, when he could only wear it while he was asleep.

She ran her fingers slowly down his, to rub over the base of his ring finger. Maybe she should surprise him with one for their next anniversary. His hand deserved something beautiful.

His fingers linked strongly with hers and pulled her into his body, holding her against him as tightly as it was possible with hands alone. A frustrating failure at tightness. "I want to hold you so much." His fingers flexed into her palms. His head bent lower toward her face. "I can't hold you, but you could hold me," he whispered with fierce longing.

Except that it would be all over for her if she did. She would press her cheek against his chest and hold on so tight and something, some chance she had sought coming here, would be lost. Her fingers returned his pressure, helplessly. She didn't want to hurt him. But the thought of giving up on her escape made her feel as if she was suffocating herself. Consciously and knowingly squeezing the pillow down over her face, to spare someone else.

Maybe they could just spend his few days here together like a honeymoon couple, the honeymoon they had never had, and then when he left she could spread back into the space for herself her vacation was supposed to offer.

Oh, was that *what it was supposed to offer?*

Except that if he moved into the bungalow, he wouldn't leave space behind him when he departed. He would leave a vast hole, and she would be the little sliver pressed against the wall, struggling to deal with his absence. An unreasoning dread filled her at the thought. "When do you have to go back?" she asked.

Daniel stiffened and stepped back from her. "What do you mean?"

"How long can you stay?"

He stared at her. His fingers, still tangled with hers, flexed too hard. "How long can *you* stay?"

She shrugged uncertainly. "Eve can probably handle the business management without me for a little while. You could always send a message to the hotel for me, if there's something you don't know how to handle." She so did not want to have to deal with damn *numbers* and personnel emergencies while she was here. She had *never* wanted to deal with them. But she probably couldn't just abandon her responsibilities indefinitely.

"*I* could send a message?" Daniel said, as if it was inconceivable that *he* should need to request any help with his own restaurant.

"You know, you don't actually know how to handle every aspect of the restaurant without me," Léa said stiffly. *Vas-y, handle the numbers and see how you like it.* But she could hardly dump that job on him on top of everything else he did.

"I know that." Anger flicked through his tone and in the flex of his hands. "But I can't send a message to you about the restaurant when we're both here."

She bit her lip.

He let go of her hands and took a hard step away from her, pivoting toward the sunset. It limned him beautifully, the gold and rose gleaming off the water, shimmering around his silhouette. He made her heart ache with longing at how beautiful he was, and for once he wasn't on a television set or in the kitchens, too busy. He was right there. She could have touched him.

But she swallowed over a lump in her throat and curled her hands into soft fists.

It was a long time before he spoke. And when he did, he still faced the sunset, a hard, beautiful silhouette. "How long are you planning to stay here, Léa?"

"I don't know," she said uneasily. And defensively: "I know it's expensive, but we can afford it."

He made a cutting gesture with one hand. "That's not the point. I'll take another consulting job to cover it, if you need me to."

Something about that hurt her so badly. "You don't think some of the money the restaurant earns might be mine, too?" she asked stiffly.

He turned sharply. "Léa, what are you *talking* about? You *manage* the place. It was *your inheritance*. Our house was your inheritance. I just meant—the consulting money is usually extra. Not something we might need to put back into the restaurant these days. I can cover a stay in the Pacific."

There was that *I* again. The truth in that *I* shouldn't hurt, but it did. She wanted him to go away now, and she felt as if, when he claimed himself as the one who would pay for it, he had just shattered her right to stay on as her own person if he left.

The sun was sinking below the horizon, its bright edge softening enough to reveal his face against it again. His mouth curved, unexpectedly. "You don't know how happy that makes me, Léa, when you gave everything to me, just handed yourself and your father's restaurant over with all that trust, to be able to say that I can pay for however long a vacation in an island resort you want."

And yet, that happiness still somehow hurt her. Her jaw thrust out a tiny bit. "Maybe *I* wanted to pay for it."

He just stared at her for a long moment. That tightness came back to his face, and he turned back toward the ocean. "Whatever you prefer, of course." They salaried both of them from the restaurant, and their salaries had always been exactly equal, a question of how to handle taxes more than anything else; the salaries themselves went straight into their joint account, which Léa managed. While spending within the restaurant had often been a subject of hot dispute, especially at the beginning when Léa worried about how tight things were and Daniel worried about quality, she didn't think they had ever really fought about personal spending. Daniel just didn't spend much, for one thing—too busy—and what little he did spend tended to be on presents he picked up on consulting trips for her. And Léa had always been very smart and careful about money, with the bulk of her expenditures going to take care of her younger siblings until her brother, the youngest, landed his first real job a year ago, meaning both were finally completely independent.

Whatever Daniel earned from *Top Chef* and consulting also went into their joint account. Léa had been the one who first started landing him those spots, before his success at them helped make him famous, but of course the money from that was more...his. His accomplishments.

"When you say you don't know how long you want to stay." Daniel's voice sounded stifled. "Are we talking about a week? Two? A month?"

A month, Léa thought with relief. A month sounded good. As if she could breathe. "Maybe."

A sharp, indrawn breath. Daniel didn't say anything again for a long time.

"How long can *you* stay?" she pressed finally, again. This place was going to feel so empty now without him.

He threw her a feral look, and then on a hard breath he suddenly jumped down into his kayak and took off, driving the paddle into the water as he headed past his bungalow and out toward the reef and the sunset.

The next morning, she didn't see Daniel at all. She kept expecting him, hesitating to head off on a walk down the beach or eat breakfast, conscious of waiting for him so that she could adapt her life around his. Until finally she went to check his bungalow and didn't find him there, although his kayak was tied there. He was probably out snorkeling or something, she thought, a little disgruntled. No problem pursuing *his* life without her.

Think, for half a second, her brain whispered. *He's here, isn't he?*

He's not pursuing his life without you. He must have dumped all kinds of obligations. He just reshaped his entire packed schedule to your whim. How could you be so self-absorbed?

But...*how could seizing a little escape for herself, after eleven years of doing everything for everyone else, be such a self-absorbed thing to do?*

She went into the main resort, filled with flowers fresh-picked that morning. A bowl of white tiare buds sat at the reception desk, and she tucked one behind her ear, the sweet scent wafting around her.

"Madame Laurier!" Tane Ehu, the manager-receptionist, brightened. "I found you paints!"

"You did?" Léa exclaimed, happy and for some reason terrified. Maybe she should never have asked about the art supplies.

"Yes, and drawing things. My cousin paints some of the art we have in the gift shop, and I talked him into letting you have some of his supplies."

"*Thank* you!" Léa said, wondering if she even remembered how to paint. Her stomach knotted stupidly. "With—with canvas and everything?" Blank canvas.

"He says he can sell that to you while he orders more supplies. I might start trying to keep some in the gift shop." He tilted his head doubtfully, a manager who had no idea how to make this beautiful place succeed. "People might like to paint here."

For a moment, Léa wanted to say, *Never mind, I don't want to take his things, it's no big deal.* She forced the urge down and her chin up. "I'll take everything he can spare. Just charge it to my room."

The manager smiled, pulling a giant worn cotton tote out from behind the rattan reception desk. A sketch book, pencils, two canvases, a selection of oils.

Léa took it and slung it over her shoulder, wincing at the friction against her skin before she transferred it back to her hand. The weight of it made her feel oddly lighter, and still afraid. "Have you seen my husband today?"

Tane slid her a curious glance but did not say anything about her husband staying in a bungalow on the opposite side of the lagoon from her. His face brightened. "He's in the kitchen! Madame Laurier, you didn't tell us your husband was a famous chef! He's helping my brother."

Léa stopped still in the kitchen door at the sight of Daniel at a counter, talking to a Polynesian man in his twenties and demonstrating something as he sliced. The other man focused on Daniel with all his attention.

Multiple plates spread out around them, clearly Daniel sampling and experimenting with what the restaurant already offered. She recognized the signs. Daniel Laurier, top chef, was going to take on this little resort's restaurant. By the time he was done with it, people would probably be renting helicopters and yachts just to come in and eat here.

She laughed, helpless affection rushing through her. He looked up, his eyes getting caught on her face, and the knife slipped off the onion and into his hand.

"*Putain,*" he told the other man. "This is what I mean about needing to keep your knives sharp."

"So you could have cut your finger off?" Léa challenged as she reached them, picking up his hand and inspecting it. The knife had hit a knuckle, leaving a bleeding nick. One of Daniel's knives would have cut through to bone.

"It never would have slid over the onion in the first place, if it had been sharp," Daniel said severely. "You know what I think about knives."

"Yes, well, I say, teach the knife skills before you make them so sharp they'll maim anyone clumsy."

"How can you teach knife skills with a dull knife?"

Since she was never in her life going to win an argument against Daniel inside a kitchen, Léa just shook her head at him, still smiling, drawing him to the nearest sink to rinse his finger. "Weren't you supposed to be taking a vacation?" she chided.

But Daniel's face did not relax in response. He gave a nominal smile in return and looked down at the hand she held in the water. "You're going to—" He took a proper look at the tote. His eyes flashed back to her face, searching. "You're going to paint?" His voice was both astonished and careful.

Léa hadn't been quite sure she had the nerve to see how much her art skills had deteriorated in the past ten years. But her chin firmed now. "Yes," she said. "I am."

Daniel came out to find her at lunch, discovering her on the beach, cursing at sand. "It gets in your oils everywhere. I need a drop cloth or something."

"Maybe they'll let you ruin a tablecloth." He stopped to study her drawing, and Léa flinched with embarrassment. Her talent sure as hell did not match his. About the only place her paintings would ever hang was in her own home. And that was on the slim chance she could manage a painting she wouldn't be mortified to look at.

"This is really nice, Léa," he said.

"Daniel. It's pathetic."

He shot her a glance. "I didn't say it was good. I've never done a damn thing that was good the first try. But I like what you're aiming for. This rustic style that's not quite primitive, but that's bright and real. You hit it best around the bungalow. Is the sunlight on the water hard to catch?"

"Yes," Léa said, heartfelt. And intensely in love with him for respecting her enough not to tell her something was good when he never, ever told anyone with any hope of being good that they had made it to that "good" before they actually had. "As you can doubtless tell."

He smiled at her. "I'm sorry, were you expecting me to feel sorry for you because you have to *practice*?"

She laughed, utterly and completely in love with him, tilting her face up to invite a kiss.

He plopped down on the sand beside her and gave it to her, long and hungry, then studied her legs, paint-splotched from propping up the canvas while she sat cross-legged. "You need an easel. Maybe I can come up with something." He frequently invented implements and put together frames to manage some impossible thing he wanted to do in the kitchens. He picked up her sketchbook and flipped it open, while she was still thinking about how nice his mouth felt on hers.

She started, spreading her fingers over her face to hide her flush as he turned past the first two sketches—failed attempts to evoke the lagoon with pencils—and came to what she had tried next, portraits. Of him. His silhouette against the sunset, because she would love to be able to paint anything half as beautiful as it had been. His face bent over a plate, as he adjusted something to perfection. That little half smile he had on *Top Chef*, which he said was always due to her.

And again, that look of his which she used to try to capture so often as a teenager, brilliant through his lashes straight at her. She had gotten far worse at drawing since she was a teenager. It made her feel sad.

Daniel drew a slow finger over his own cheekbone in the drawing and looked at her. "Léa."

She blushed and squeezed her fingers together so that they shut her eyes.

He kissed her right between her hands, her lips the one spot on her face left unshielded. Not touching her hands themselves, not trying to pull away her shield.

Then he spread out a couple of pareos on the sand and unzipped the soft cooler he had brought, watching her with bright eyes as she sipped juice made fresh from island grapefruits and barely sweetened with a secret touch of rosemary-infused syrup, then chilled to perfection. Her eyes met his as she sipped it, savoring his pleasure in offering it to her as much as the drink itself. "Thank you," she murmured, and he smiled, turning back to the cooler.

Pulling out first pork sliced fine and intricately paired with slivers of avocado and pineapple. Then an elegant strata of mango and papaya and passion fruit, layered in perfect little ripples in a whiskey glass he must have stolen from the bar.

Sometimes she just loved him so much. His compulsion and his hunger and his pleasure in creating this and offering it to her. The way he took what he saw and tasted around him and refined it into something so perfect. She slipped her hand around his and kissed it, pressing a smile into his knuckles.

He turned his hand over and caressed her cheek as he let it fall slowly back down to the pareo. He watched her a while as she ate, a little smile on his mouth, and then relaxed onto his back, tucking his hands under his head.

"You're not hungry?"

He shrugged.

"You nibbled in the kitchen."

Another shrug. "Some."

"Daniel, you were kayaking all day yesterday. You can't survive on tasting sessions."

He closed his eyes, the palms above them shading his face with here and there a brush of sun. She proffered him a sliver of mango, and he turned his head towards her immediately, lips parting willingly, kissing her fingers as he took it. But he didn't sit up and reach for food for himself.

"You can't possibly be snubbing *this* food. You made it."

The faint tightening of his mouth. "I wasn't snubbing the other food, Léa."

She frowned at him.

Silence. Daniel locked his hands behind his head and looked at the palm fronds. "I can't eat when I'm stressed," he said at last, in what seemed an effort at evenness.

And eleven years—eleven years—of her trying so hard to feed him up as he prepped for something brutal, some championship or *Top Chef* competition, and of him swearing her food was delicious while he picked at it with a faint expression of revulsion...eleven years suddenly got put in a radically different perspective.

She stared at him. He gazed at the palm-filtered sky, his expression stoic somehow, determined.

"You're stressed?" she asked cautiously. They were on a deserted beach, on a remote Pacific island, eating tropical delicacies that had just been made by one of the world's top chefs and watching the waves. She wasn't stressed. She had been thinking to hell with this attempt to discover a space for herself, that she wanted to curl up against his chest and not have any space at all.

Daniel's expression didn't change, but the tendons shifted in his forearms, as if something had happened to the hands hidden under his head. After a minute, he said, "I am enjoying this. Every single second of the waves, and the heat, and—you. I can't remember the last time we spent so much time together. But I do know, Léa, that you don't want me to be here, and that you're just too sweet to kick me out. Plus, you can't. I won't go. So—yes," that compression of his voice that made it so low, "I am stressed."

"I don't want to kick you out!" she protested. But she really wasn't sure she wanted him to be here either. *I went away for me, and I don't want this to become about somebody else.*

"That's what I said," Daniel replied much too evenly. She wondered how exactly he had developed that evenness. She had seen the ability grow, over time, from the intense teenager who sometimes had no idea how to impose himself without anger to back him up. She wondered suddenly if it was still growing, if right now he was putting his ability to stay even to a great trial of strength.

"And there's nothing to stress over, Daniel. This is not—honestly, this is just about me."

Under that evenness, his jaw line was so tense. That tension reminded her of their wedding day, oddly. That taut profile beside her in the church, how straight his shoulders had been and how high his head. "All right," he said. "But I'm just going to stick around, because I'm interested in things that are all about you."

Chapter Nine

D aniel's temper kept flicking him. He wanted to shout at her, *What the fuck do you think, that I can eat when you're saying it's all about you? As if you like it that way? As if you could get used to it? I'm the one who's supposed to be the superstar, and I would* never *say that about* me.

But he didn't shout because they had gotten past their tempestuous fights as teenagers trying to handle marriage and one of the world's top restaurants, all at once. Other than occasional irritability, they hadn't had a proper fight in years. He had learned to control his temper, and Léa—well, other than to give him a little leeway when he was clearly stressed sometimes, she hadn't had that much to learn how to do. She had always been a sweet, infectiously happy kind of person.

He missed that infectious happiness for him right now so much that he was growing desperate, his stomach pure knots. It was a wonder he hadn't cut his own finger off when he finally got a glimpse of that delight in him that morning.

And...he barely even saw her anymore as it was. How much less of him did she need, to let it be "all about her"? What the fuck had he not done right?

Once she had stopped traveling with him and started sleeping so damn much, they had pretty much been reduced to business contact at the restaurant and when he woke her up at one in the morning. And at the restaurant, he admittedly was not always at his best. Difficult, intense, driving everyone, all the time. Well...except that he *was* at his best—one of the best in the world—the only best of himself he had ever had time to be.

He sat up. "Léa—"

"Daniel," she said at the same time, her head cocked, and he caught himself. On the alert for any fucking clue he could get as to what was going on. Her eyes searched his. "Have you ever regretted marrying me?"

It hit him like a bomb blast, no noise in his head, too much noise. His stomach already knotted, it was all he could do not to roll over and be sick. "*No,*" he said, strangled. Fuck. Fuck, what was she regretting?

Handing all her life, her inheritance, her sweet, beautiful self into the hands of a nineteen-year-old who hadn't a clue how to be worth all that?

"It was so much work, at the beginning," she said. "You were never sorry?"

"God, no, Léa." He pressed his forehead into his fingers, shielding his face. And, *It's still so much work. I can't breathe for how much work I'm doing. I never see you.* "You—you were? Sorry?"

"*No!*" she sounded startled, and his head whipped up.

"Then what the fuck are we talking about?" he challenged harshly. "Why did you bring it up?"

"I—I just wondered," she said awkwardly, pleating her hands. "I mean—I know you were always ambitious and wanted the restaurant, but I just—"

"You know *what?*" If it had been a bomb blast before, he didn't even have words for this.

Her eyes widened. She scooted backward in the sand. "I mean, I just—Daniel, *you* know how you went after me, as soon as you saw the chef's daughter."

He was going to be physically sick. They might have to remove his stomach to let him live. "I went after the—" And then he exploded. If he could have touched her without hurting her, he might have thrown her somewhere. As it was, he lunged to all fours, digging fists into the sand to squeeze it, face into hers, making her topple back warily. "I went after you," he said between his teeth. He wanted to *bite* that stunned mouth so near his. Bite it hard, so she bled as much as she had just made him. "Even though I thought your father would fire me when he found out. I can't—" Him leaning over her against a wall of jasmine, slipping a flower behind her ear. The giddy pleasure of knowing it was working, knowing she was tempted by him. Shy, pretty, happy, eager...all for him. "You thought I was after the *restaurant*?"

"Not like that! Not—using me or anything. But it must have been part of my appeal. Subconsciously."

"Léa." He needed to tear something. Himself. Anything. "I admired your father. He was a huge man. It was a privilege to work for him. The first day I saw you, when you came back from that summer art class in Italy, I thought, *Don't be an idiot. You can't go after her. He'll fire you in two seconds.* And the second day I saw you—I went after you."

She sat on her butt, clinging to the sand, blinking at him as if he had just told her the Earth was actually a triangle. "Oh, *putain*," he realized, the hurt so violent he didn't know how to hold it. "You think I *married* you for the restaurant, too, don't you?"

"Not *consciously*! You're not like that!"

"You don't think I was *conscious* of what that restaurant meant? I was *nineteen years old*. I hadn't even risen to *second* yet. For my *career*, I needed to abandon ship like everyone else did, find another three-star chef to train under. But what the fuck would have happened to all your inheritance, if I took a different job? I married you because *no one* would have given an eighteen-year-old and her *boyfriend* any chance at all. I married you because losing your father tore you apart, and I wanted to fill that hole. I married you because I loved you, but fuck, Léa, we would probably have dated longer, until I was better established and you finished university, if your father hadn't died, you know that." His teeth clenched. The words slammed out of him. "How can you not know that?"

How could he have given his whole life to her, and she not realize it?

She sat staring at him, a sandy hand pressed to her mouth. Her eyes glittered, wet. Oh, fuck, not again. He could not *stand* it when she cried. He could barely even stand to be in the same room with her if she was in tears, like he had to shred his way out of his own skin.

"Léa." He came up off his hands onto his knees, away from her. Sand spilled slowly from the fist he forced to open, as he fought for his breathing, labored and slow. "I married you because I thought you needed me. It never occurred to me to ask, back then, if you loved me, too."

He stood. From his second fist, sand fell in a heavy clump. "I guess part of me knew you did, and part of me could never have believed I deserved it."

And he really had to get out of here. He headed off down the beach.

It took him a long time to walk himself into any kind of calm. Walk and swim and walk some more. He didn't come back until the sun was setting, an early equatorial night. The light angled across the water, astonishingly beautiful. How had he gone all his life without seeing this?

High up on the sand, someone had drawn giant letters. D-A-N...he stopped, his hands in his pockets. His name, enormous, encircled by a heart that was just starting to lose its tip to the tide.

All that anger still knotting his chest and his belly loosened, despite itself, his whole world brightening. She was just so sweet. He could imagine her dragging a stick, leaving it for him, an apology for letting him pour his whole life into her hands and still doubting he loved her. Or maybe just to remind him that she loved him, and that was the thing that mattered most.

Well, she was right about that.

But he didn't go knock on her bungalow. She probably still wanted space.

Maybe he wanted some space, too.

He didn't come back all day, and at night, after she finally saw his shadow move in the window of his bungalow, Léa slumped in her own window, staring out at the ocean horizon, her arms wrapped around herself, remembering his face. The shock of it. Those brilliant, beautiful eyes, that intense, driven face, the relentless man—all wide open with hurt.

He must love you more than you ever even began to guess.

How could that be?

The driven nineteen-year-old who wanted to become the very best. He hadn't taken on the restaurant because it was his dream come true, he had taken it on because *she* was his dream, and he was willing to take her on, no matter how much she hampered him in the pursuit of that best?

Being the best was what drove Daniel. His absolute, dominant need.

He loved her, she had never doubted that. But he *had* to be the best. Right?

Top Chef, her brain whispered, as if she was missing something still. *He said he didn't want to do Top Chef.*

His fingertips touching his jaw, tracing a memory of her kisses...

She pressed her forehead into her palms, knotting her fingers through her hair, not even sure what to do anymore. She was heart-soaringly enraptured by the thought that he might love her so much. And yet, how could she soar on that love when her wings felt atrophied?

Daniel, she thought, to his shadow across the lagoon on his dock, *I didn't mean to hurt you. I* don't *mean to hurt you.*

I don't mean to hurt us.

And because of that, she would make it up to him. Tomorrow she would. She would stop trying to defend her space. Exhaustion swept her at the thought, and she tried to fight it with images of Daniel. Angry, hurt, too tense to eat, sand spilling from an unclenched fist...each image she used to fight her own fatigue seemed only to increase it. *I love you, I love you, my wonderful white-knight hero, who fought every dragon of the food world. For me.*

The burns, and the critics, and the brutal unrelenting work, and the hostility of the whole world toward two teenagers with hubris. There had been so many dragons.

If he did all that for her, how could she possibly have the right to want still more of something for herself?

And yet...*what if it was even more important than I realized, that this little escape be really, truly...all about me?*

Chapter Ten

When Daniel came out of his bungalow just before sunrise, Léa was sitting cross-legged on his wooden deck, a quiet, dark figure in the gray-blue light, the first hint of gold sliding over the water.

She reached up a hand, pulling him down to sit beside her. Then she leaned her head against his chest and wrapped her arms around him, not saying anything, just pressing into him.

His stomach relaxed for the first time since the waterfall. He slipped an arm very carefully around her. "How's the back?" *How are you? How are we? Is everything okay now?*

She nodded against his chest without speaking, which he took to mean it was better. Maybe that a lot of things were better. He checked under her top, another tunic from the gift shop. Skin starting to peel. So, safe to the touch.

He tightened his arm abruptly, and then, control snapped, it went tighter, and tighter, until she made a little sound of protest. His own skin flinched and begged him to stop, but that he could ignore. He had had worse burns than the sunburn he had earned spending the entire day brooding on the beach and in the water. Burns from everything from hot oil to liquid nitrogen to—the worst—molten caramel. Just not all over every inch of his chest and back and arms at once. With her arms wrapped around those burns, squeezing them.

Still, it was worth it. She was the one who protested his tight hold.

"*Pardon.*" He loosened his hold, breathing deeply. It was the first time since he had discovered her missing that he felt like he could breathe. The sky flushed pink, the sun reaching the horizon on the other side of the island.

"Spend the day with me?" she said.

Oh, thank God. A smile kicked across his face, and Léa's brightened in relief. His stomach loosened enough to point out that it was pretty damn hungry and could they eat soon. It made him feel a little giddy. After all that anger and hurt and that desperate knot of fear. "If I can make love to you until you beg for mercy, I might be persuaded," he told her, with a slow sideways smile. "Otherwise, I should go help Moea in the kitchens. This place is in serious need of a restaurant that can draw guests."

She blinked and looked down. Then she glanced up at him sideways and away.She didn't say anything, but a slow blush climbed up her cheeks, like the flush on the horizon. Exactly like when they were teenagers, she had always been too embarrassed to say what she wanted out loud, at least until they got a lot more into the heat of things.

And just like when they were teenagers, if in the end he didn't get to make love to her and just got his hands under her shirt, he would probably still manage to be happy as hell.

"You're the one sunburned today," she reproved him. Although she was tempted. He had tried to tempt her often enough to know when it was working, and it always made heat press through his veins.

"Back and front, too." He went ahead and pulled off his shirt, using the moment it passed over his face to hide an unusual self-satisfaction. Sometimes it paid to work like a dog at an extremely physical job, too stressed to eat enough. One thing he had was definition. He liked the rare occasions when he got to make love to her in the daylight, where she could get a proper look at that definition, because he liked reminding her that he had more things going for him than being her superhero chef. Sometimes it was nice to be—just the man she liked to touch.

He twisted a little, ostensibly so she could view the sunburn both back and front, but really because it flexed his abs and made her eyes track down his body and her pupils eat up a bit more of her pretty gold-brown eyes. He leaned into her, savoring the way her eyes stroked up his whole body as he grew closer, until they caught on his. He lowered his voice, a husk of sex all through it: "This time *you* won't be able to touch *me*. You won't even be able to fight me off, while I do what I want to you."

Good God, this tropical island vacation must be going to his head. Or maybe it was just the fact that she had finally wrapped her arms around him, like she was glad to hold him again. He hadn't felt so— boyishly cocky since they were teenagers, and he leaned over her on a hillside, and saw her eyes widen, and knew she was going to let him kiss her because she just couldn't resist any more than he could.

Things had just gotten so intense, not long after that. He hadn't had any energy left for boyish cockiness. He had needed it all for hard-driven arrogance, the refusal to let anyone or anything keep him down when she needed him to rise.

She drew a breath, like someone making sure she had enough oxygen for a plunge. "What if I just run my nails very lightly down that sunburn?" she managed, her own voice husky even while she tried for dryness. "Would that fight you off?"

He laughed and picked up her hand to kiss the inside of her wrist. Her pulse jumped under his fingers. "As if you could be that mean. But my butt is free. Unlike you, I kept mine covered." He slipped her hand right under his waistband, curving it around one cheek. "You can grab that as much as you want." He brought his mouth right to her ear. "And even pull hard."

She twisted her head into his neck, a slow, sensual nuzzle, and it hit him with an erotic jolt: she was savoring his scent. *Oh, putain.* That was so—hot. And so deliciously love-filled and sweet, all at once. "At least let me put aloe on you," she murmured.

"Mmm, now you're getting kinky." He pulled her to her feet with him. "I'll tell you what. Let's do my idea first, about making you beg for mercy, and then you can put nasty stuff on me that no one would want to touch. When I need a break from your insatiable demands." He was enjoying being outrageous far more than he had ever had time to realize he could.

She laughed helplessly, that old delight in him all twined with arousal. Heat surged higher in him. "Daniel, the sooner you put some on the better."

"Well. I guess you'll have to wear me out fast."

He drew her into her bungalow to pack a bag for the day. Getting inside it without any of her strange, terrifying resistance relaxed him yet another degree. Everything was going to be just fine. He could breathe again. They had cleared up a misunderstanding, and she was sorry, and she still loved him, and it was all going to be okay. It hurt still, yes, that she could ever have thought that he had married her for the *restaurant.* Ever have thought it for one second, let alone as the backdrop of her opinion of him for eleven fucking years.

But...he could get past that. He was—not difficult, with her. He never had been. A heart in the sand, her head pressed against his chest in apology—

He would do anything, for her. For that. A claim that had been tested, over and over, after her father's death, when he had had to make good on all his claims. He had, indeed, done anything. Everything. Over and over and over.

These past few months, when she had stopped traveling with him, he had begun to feel stretched beyond bearing. But maybe this was a lesson to him. He could stand the pace, after all. As long as she was there as his reason.

When she held onto him so tightly, his world re-stabilized. He could do the rest, as long as he didn't feel as if the entire granite base on which his world was built had just turned into a sandcastle on some tropical beach, with the tide coming in.

He tried to pack up her art supplies for their walk, and a shadow shifted across her face. "They'll be a pain to carry, don't worry about them."

He straightened slowly, the tote in hand, something uneasy twisting through his sense of relief. "I don't mind."

"Just let it go." She looked oddly tense, like when she had to fire someone at the restaurant, or those early years when she had tried to do their taxes on her own. The first time she had tried to do them, at eighteen, he had found her sitting over the papers crying.

It had about killed him, and he had gone straight back into the kitchens and worked all night, experimenting with new dishes, determined to wow the critics so much that they could finally afford to pay her father's old accountant again. He wondered suddenly if, instead, he should have stepped into the office and given her a hug. That would have been so much harder to do, though, face her tears helplessly.

"I'll just carry them," he said. "You might change your mind." *Putain,* she had better not give up on something just because it didn't turn out perfectly the first time. Not after the way he had lived *his* life.

81

"You don't need to have a strap rubbing against your shoulder," she snapped.

His eyebrows went up a little. Léa could get snappish under pressure at the restaurant, but not in many other circumstances. It was more his style, to be honest, and usually, unfortunately, directed a bit at her, his reason for taking on so many stressors.

"How about a sketchbook and some pencils?" He tucked them into a backpack with their lunch. "Here. You can carry them." He slipped the backpack onto her shoulders and was deeply offended when she accepted that matter-of-factly, not with the startled indignation he had expected. "Okay, give it back."

"No, I'm fine." She tried to tighten the shoulder straps for her smaller build. "Put the aloe in there, too, all right?"

"Léa, give me that." He pulled on the pack.

She tightened her hands around the straps. "It will hurt your shoulders! It's your own fault for not putting sunscreen on."

"So I'll carry it in one hand. It's not that heavy. Léa—" He worked his fingers under hers, prying a hand away from the straps. She locked it back around as soon as he shifted his efforts to the other hand.

"I'm *fine.*" Her mouth set stubbornly.

He shifted in frustration, profoundly uncomfortable.

"That will teach you not to wear sunscreen," she informed him.

It would indeed. The sight of his wife carrying their load made everything about him itch to right the situation. "You know what? Let's just stay here." He pushed her face-down onto her bed, and while her hands were trapped under her weight, flicked the straps completely undone and pulled the backpack off her, setting it to the side. Fast hands came with the profession. "This would be a beautiful place to spend a day out of the sun."

It would, too. Like his, her bungalow had a little glass section in the floor through which they could watch the fish. She had closed the shutters facing the resort's main area, for privacy, but all the other wide windows were thrown open to the wind and sea. Staff from the resort had set a bouquet of tiare buds on the nightstand, so that the sweet, rich scent filled the space, wafted gently back and forth by the sea breezes. Rattan furniture emphasized the vacation feel of the room, as did the great blue hibiscus quilted onto her white bedspread.

It was an exquisite haven of shade, for someone whose torso burned all over, utterly restful and open to the sea.

Léa wiggled over onto her back, her gaze skating down and up the length of him. She didn't try to sit up.

Heat swelled in him, slow and steady. Oh, so she had liked that, had she? Being pushed down onto the bed?

They needed to take vacations more often. Who knew she had so many other moods than the ones at one in the morning and the ones on a lazy Monday afternoon?

Temper surged, unexpectedly, that deep well of anger that he kept accidentally tapping into, ever since he had come home to find her message. Married more than ten years, and yet he had barely had a chance to learn his own wife's moods. *I'm not doing this anymore*, he thought suddenly, an abrupt about-face from his resolution of only moments before. *When we get home, things are going to change.*

I don't care. We'll face it. I'll handle it. I'll make *her see there is something else to me.*

He came down onto the bed above her, pulling her body lengthwise. Her eyes darkened, the gold gleaming in the brown like the shine of treasure in the depths of a cave. She didn't say anything, but her lips parted, and her head turned to follow his movements, so that his access to that mouth was always easy.

His lips curved. She was in his favorite mood. Tempted. Tempted by him. He had learned it as a teenager, learned to push it, to build her temptation into something she couldn't resist. *Yes, I can make you see me again. Make you want me more than whatever the fuck you want on this island.*

Slanting his body across the bedspread, so that none of it touched her, he wove his hands through her hair and kissed her.

She responded instantly, yielding and then hungry. "I've missed you," she whispered, her hands tangling in his hair, shaping his head to her. "I've missed you. I don't know what to do."

What to do? That sounded as if there was some problem that—he started to lift his head, but she tightened her hold, pulling his mouth back into hers. And he forgot about her words for just a second, just one more moment, because she was letting him kiss her again, really kiss her, stretched out on her bed kiss her, and that meant everything would be fine, it had all been a false alarm, everything would be absolutely fine...

He sank himself into the kisses until she was wild with them, petting his head frantically, until the muscles of his arms ached with tension, but he held himself off her, touching her only with his mouth and his hands in her hair.

"Yes." Her whisper was so soft only he could ever have heard it. A breath just for him. "Daniel...fuck my mouth."

Hot pleasure surged through him. He loved it when he could make her talk like that. Mostly when he got home late—well, mostly she made a sleepy mumble, and he played with her hair and drew a finger down her back, and if that failed to lure her out of sleep, he let it go, completely incapable of forcing her awake for his own pleasure. Instead, he slipped an arm around her and nuzzled his face into her neck, letting the scent of her ease him off his adrenalin. In fact, once when she had changed shampoos, he had had to beg her to change back, so he could get to sleep.

But other than staying asleep, the next most likely reaction was drowsy, pliant, welcoming love-making, and God, but he loved that, too.

But once in a while, something dark and urgent rose up in her, freed by sleep, dreams, and the dark, and it drove him wild, although it made her blush in the mornings.

She had never let that dark, wild thing rise up in her in the daylight before.

Her fingers hurt his hair, pulling his mouth into hers urgently. "Fuck my mouth," she murmured again, such sweet, hot begging.

So he did. Not touching anything but her head, her hair, he ravaged her with long hot strokes until she was shivering all over, making little hungry, yearning sounds that soothed seven days of tension out of him and replaced it with another kind of tension entirely. Triumphant, victor's tension. She was his. She was still utterly his.

Her hands kept sliding down to his sunburned shoulders, a flinch of pain in the midst of pleasure, and he loved the guilty way she would suddenly realize and her hands would fly away from him. And come back to his hair, frantically shaping his head.

And then forget again.

"Here," he said. "Let me help." He took her hands and locked them, powerless, above her head, lifting himself to look down at that incredible view.

The bones and angles and curves of her, all twisting and shivering and melting with need. Trapped by him. All his.

He drew one hand down the length of her, delicately, tracing from collarbone straight over one nipple, all the way to the crease of her thigh, and she gasped and shivered.

He bent his head and whispered in her ear: "I'll fuck you any way I like."

She moaned, her wrists twisting in his hold. He bore them down into the bed, and her hips arched up instead, seeking his. *Take me!*

Yes, take her! his body shouted.

But, of course, he could control that, too. It was worth it, to control his body a little longer so he could savor the joy of controlling hers.

He wasn't sure he had ever realized how much he *could* control hers. Always so hungry for her, he had never even tried.

It took one hell of a lot of arrogance to have a woman begging for you and not seize your chance before she changed her mind. She made him arrogant. In fact, every bit of arrogance he had came from his need for her and her pride in him.

But she had never before made him arrogant enough to make her beg. "I love you," he whispered, cupping her sex.

"Daniel, please." She opened her eyes. "I want to touch you."

"I know." He traced the lips of her sex with one thumb, watching her face. "I wanted to touch you yesterday. And the day before. And the whole time I was in Japan without you. And when I came back to find you missing, with nothing but a damn phone message and your own phone lying by your bed. I wanted to touch you, Léa." His hand tightened on her wrists. "And I couldn't."

"I didn't mean—" His thumb slipped inside her, and she gasped and twisted, her words fracturing. "Coming here was nothing to do w—"

He drove one finger straight into her body, hard and deep, and she shut up on a gasp, her eyes going wide. "Yes, you've mentioned," he said between his teeth, holding her speared there. "Several times. That it had nothing to do with me. Well, guess what, Léa." As her surprised muscles figured out what they wanted to do with his finger and squeezed around it, he pulled it out—away from her sex entirely. Coming up her body to take one of her nipples and twist it very gently. "*This does.*"

Her head tossed restlessly, her mouth, her sex, her body all open and begging, everywhere. "Daniel."

"Yes, say my name." He brought his mouth to her other nipple, pressing his thigh up between hers. "I want to be all *you* can think about, all *you* can do, all *you* can be."

He lifted his head to emphasize the words and saw confusion flicker even through her arousal, tangle with it in her eyes. "But—you already *are!*" she protested desperately. "Daniel, I can't—please don't ask for *more.*"

What? But he couldn't think about that now. He didn't want to think about it. He wanted to make her his, over and over his again, like he had claimed her on the beach, like he had claimed her at the waterfall. *Not* like she had claimed him, which had left him feeling vulnerable and...vulnerable. Two full days later, he still could not grapple with the concept of Léa on her knees before him.

He was supposed to be *her* knight, and...he was supposed to be in control.

"*Say my name,*" he said between his teeth, shifting his hips between hers.

Her eyes caught his above her. And widened, hers very dark, hiding the gold. Her body stopped twisting in hunger, and one long gasp moved through it. "Daniel," she said quietly and very firmly. Asserting her own claim.

Or accepting his.

And then suddenly her face lit in that old delight in him, as if the sun rose and set on him, as if he was her world. As if she had remembered that. "I love you," she whispered, her face so happy, and he was inside her before he even realized what he was doing.

A thrust so hard and so sudden that she gave a half-laugh and a gasp. Her smile dissolved, her eyes falling shut, and her muscles closed around him.

Yes.

He was home, he was where he belonged, *nothing* mattered more right now than her body taking him.

He realized he had released her wrists only when one of her hands jerked guiltily away from his sunburned back—he hadn't even felt the pain. She slid both hands down to his butt and sank them in hard, as if to remind herself not to let them slide anywhere else.

Mmm. "Nice," he breathed, leaning down closer to her, trying to keep watching her face, but his own focus kept shattering, dissolving, sinking back into his own body and her hold on him.

"You have to know I love you," she breathed, her hands flexing into him, her thighs wrapping around him, her inner muscles squeezing, as if everything about her was a message. *Putain*, but he loved the way she communicated. "You have to."

"I know it *now*." Easing out and finding home again, always a home, always a welcome, always her body tightening, her hands gripping, her head tossing. "Like this."

Her eyebrows flexed together, and her eyes opened again, but he slipped one hand under her hips to pull her into him closer, and her lashes fell back against her cheeks.

He leaned very low and close to her. "I know it all the time," he whispered. "Léa. All the time." It was what kept him going. What drove him to please her, even when that was the very thing that kept him so far from her so much. And what had thrown him into a flat panic when he had found her gone and realized she had been slipping through his fingers for months, like water he was trying too hard to hold. Panicked as if he literally would be wiped out of existence without that love.

A smile ghosted across her face and disappeared under her own arousal, her focus on sensation. Her lashes so heavy on her cheeks. He watched them flutter with each thrust, glorying in the way her fingers dug into his muscles.

He got lost in it, slipping his hand down between their bodies to make sure she was lost, too. "I love you," he whispered. "I love you." As they both came. His a hard dominant stamp of possession, and hers an utter yielding.

Chapter Eleven

The cool aloe slopped on his hot back, and he hissed and turned his head on his arms, offering her a sleepy smile. His chest and stomach hurt to lie on, too, but he hadn't slept properly for a week, and he was entirely ready to doze off. Until the aloe woke him up again.

"You should have put some on last night," Léa chided.

He hadn't had any in his room. And anyway, he didn't take care of himself much. Léa was the one who took care of him. Bandaged his wounds, kissed them, cooed over them. His mother had died young, and his father had been a good father, taking him camping and to the beach and spending time with him, but he had also been of the *Tough it up, that's life* school.

The first time seventeen-year-old Léa had spotted a burn on his hand, clucked over it, and hauled out the BurnEase and the blue bandages chefs always used, he had thought he had died and gone to heaven. He had yielded all the care of himself over to her in giddy delight. She did it so much better, and it felt so much sweeter.

He fought the battles, and she healed the wounds. It worked for him.

A quick sudden spasm of that old knot he thought was loosened. *Is it not working for her?*

No, but everything was fine now. He just had to get to the bottom of what had made her disappear like that, so that he didn't spend every future consulting trip with his stomach in knots, braced against that vast void-like terror of finding her not home again. He just wanted to make sure that would never, ever happen again. And then it would all be fine.

She was his. He had gotten her back, taken her completely. She was all his again.

At the gentle nudge of her hand, he rolled obediently over onto the big towel she had provided for that purpose, flinching as his sticky, painful back connected with it. And flinching again as the gooey stuff connected with his chest. *Putain*, but he hated that feeling. Still, the hand stroking it made it better. He loved Léa's hands. They were so much smaller than his, because she was smaller, but when a man had a chance to hold one and play with it and really focus on it—as he did sometimes on plane trips, when he was tired of working, or on those lazy Monday afternoons—he could see how she had such long fingers for the size of her hands, capable and strong and delicate, too, hands to grip a paintbrush or a man, or help her brother and sister with their school projects, or make her siblings' new apartments beautiful when they set out on their own, or set perfect tables when they were short-staffed, or any of the million things he had seen them do in the past twelve years.

His favorite thing for them to do was to grip a man, of course. He smiled and caressed a hand up her forearm to her elbow, the closest he could get to kissing one of her hands when it was covered with so much goo.

She sent him that shy smile of hers. It was funny how sometimes she could still be so shy with him. He liked it. But sometimes he wondered about it.

But then, part of him still felt profoundly shy with her, and he didn't think she even guessed it. "Love you," he murmured out loud, to cover even a hint of that shyness, which was not part of his I'll-be-your-hero role, and her eyes brightened.

Yes, everything was just fine. He was the luckiest man in the damn world.

"To think if my father hadn't insisted, I would have become a mechanic," he murmured. "He was right about a lot of things, Papa."

"A—*mechanic*?" Léa said in utter astonishment.

Had he never even mentioned that to her before? "Or stayed in school and studied, I don't know, literature or something. He wanted me to do something practical. And once I picked the culinary apprenticeship, he wouldn't let me quit."

"You wanted to *quit*?"

Well, it was nice to know he had grown so much that she couldn't believe in the smaller him. "It was tough, to be suddenly cut off from every single friend I had. You know—no nights, no weekends. And I had a good friend who was doing the mechanic training. And, I mean, I liked motorcycles and beautiful cars as much as the next teenager. I was only fifteen, Léa. But Papa—it's not fair to say he wouldn't *let* me quit. But he argued adamantly that a man didn't quit when things were hard. He just worked harder, to turn what he did into something exceptional."

Léa brought one sticky hand to her mouth, staring at him.

"So I did turn it into something exceptional." He shrugged. And if he didn't quit then, there was nothing else in life he was ever going to quit. As an only child whose mother was dead, his friends had been vitally important to him. The sudden isolation had been horrible. "And then I met you. And I knew my father had been right." She had been worth the loss of all his other friends. She had been worth honing himself into a bright and shining star.

He was born to do that, really—driven, dominant, intense, perfectionist. To her yielding, sweet warmth. It had felt like the match made in heaven to *him*.

He had even felt perfect for her, too. He had, after all, the ideal career for the daughter of a three-star chef, a girl who had grown up thinking that making wonders out of food was the epitome of what a man could be.

"Literature, hunh." She tilted her head. "I'm trying to imagine you as a professor." Her head angled to the other side. "Or restoring some old car."

He blinked and pushed himself up on one elbow, curiously. She didn't seem turned off by either image.

As if he could have been whatever he wanted to be and still had her.

His insides seemed to whoosh out of him in some gasping freefall plunge into the surreal.

She smiled a little, at whatever images were playing in her head. "You know, you look gorgeous no matter what you do," she told him and slid off the bed to go wash her hands in the bathroom.

He stared after her, all bearings lost. The thought that she might have loved him still, if he had been a professor or a mechanic instead of a top chef—he couldn't even process that. Possibly because he couldn't imagine himself being either of those things anymore. Being a superstar chef was so completely and utterly all he was. Not a father, barely a husband, barely a son to his own father whom he saw so infrequently now, just a chef, chef, chef. So damn good at it. So unbearably, intensely good at it.

He lay back down on the bed, staring at the ceiling, and heard the shower run, briefly.

Hmm. He looked down his own body, realizing suddenly that they might need to have a discussion. Léa wasn't on the pill. She had tried a couple different versions of it, long ago, and hated them, and he had hated them, too, the way they took his Léa's moods and changed her into someone different. The first one, with her increased aggression and her decreased interest in sex, had driven him frantic, and the second one...the third time in three days that she burst into tears over something utterly stupid, he had begged her to stop using it. And since then, he had always taken responsibility for contraception, and if that was a little less sure of a method, well—they were married, and he supposed on his end he had always assumed that if an accident did occur, they would adjust to the consequences and that Léa would be a gloriously wonderful mother. And he would figure out a way to tell her that he couldn't keep this pace anymore as a father, that he, too, deserved to spend time with his family.

None of which made him any less of a bastard to have ignored his responsibilities on this particular occasion. It hadn't been a conscious decision, but he wasn't a careless man, and he knew damn well what his subconscious had been trying to do.

Lock her back up to him. Make sure she wouldn't even think about slipping away.

Putain, articulated like that in his head it made him seem—vile. Léa could have reminded him, he thought defensively. It wouldn't be the first time she had to whisper *don't forget*. So why hadn't she this time? Just lost in that trust that she gave to him so easily, or was her subconscious trying to do something, too?

He grimaced, running his hands over his face as he heard the shower shut off. Yes, they needed to have a discussion, and *putain*, why did it seem like such a dangerous one?

Coming out of the bathroom, wrapped in a blue hibiscus pareo, Léa grinned at the sight of Daniel on his back with one arm thrown over his face and aloe glistening on his chest. He so hated that stuff.

He had such a gorgeous body, though. It was a damn waste to feel it mostly at one in the morning. They needed to take more vacations. Do more things where she could just stop and enjoy the view of him. A mechanic, hunh. It was oddly easy to imagine it. He would have ended up one of those mechanics who made one-off models for Ferrari auto shows. Or, seeking greater independence, started his own custom-built motorcycle business and ended up with a television show following him around as he turned old plates from the Eiffel Tower into new works of chopper art. Professor was more of a stretch, but it wasn't a bad one: the thought of him quieter, more cerebral, all that drive poured into his intellect, until he probably would have become the next Sartre. He might not have ended up with quite the same gorgeous definition in his body, but then again, knowing Daniel, he would be quite capable of becoming Sartre while running triathlons on the side. Still, imagining him with a slightly geekier physique made her smile.

She stretched out on the bed beside him, cuddling her head against one folded arm, pretending she was a professor's arty wife, maybe an art professor herself. Letting the vision lull her, content to drift toward sleep with him even though it wasn't even ten a.m. yet. It was that kind of day, and the bungalow that kind of spot, soft and shady and at peace, filled with sweet scents and the lullaby of waves.

And if she thought too much past *him* and *them*, tried to think about *her*, she felt tired again. So she pushed herself out of her mind, in order to dwell in the more important pleasures of the moment.

Daniel rolled to his side and propped himself on one elbow just as her lashes were drifting closed. Her eyes flickered back open enough to be caught by the brilliance of his, very intent, and for some reason she wanted to squeeze her eyes shut again.

"In answer to your question the other day," he said, just before her lashes reached her cheeks. "Yes. I would like for us to have kids."

Her eyes flared wide open, her contentment gone as if he had stabbed straight through it and through her, impaling her to a wall. Oh, *God*. She had known this was coming. She should have known. She was nearing thirty. And she wanted to run *screaming*, please *no, no, no, I can't, I can't. Daniel—not more.*

He was over her in a second, grabbing her shoulder as she started to roll out of bed, holding her to the mattress. "*What?*" he said between his teeth. "*Why?* Léa. Tell me why you look like that, at the thought of my kids."

She jerked a little on her shoulder, and her heart rose up in her, strangling her with tears. Oh, those damn tears. "It's nothing to do with yo—" The tears spilled out, only this time not a quiet secret, this time something ragged and painful.

"God damn it." He flung himself out of bed and to the nearest open window, silhouetting himself against azure ocean and a coast of tawny volcanic sand and verdant green. "Now my kids have nothing to do with me?" He reached up to grasp the window frame.

Léa sat up and curled over her crossed legs, trying to stop crying. "I'm sorry, it's so stupid, I don't know what's wrong with me."

He hung his head, gripping the frame until his knuckles turned white, and watched her. "Léa." His voice ground, processed with great effort. "You're killing me."

"*Why?*" she cried suddenly, frantically. "I told you I just needed a little break. I told you I just wanted to get away on my own for a few days. I told you I love you still. *Why is this so wrong?* We've been married for over ten years, and I've never taken a break once!"

His hand flexed until it was a wonder the frame didn't rip right off. "Neither have I," he said low, harshly.

"But you *wanted* that! My God, Daniel. I know you said you did it for me, but you're the one who kept driving, long past any reasonable success. You're never satisfied! You always have to do more!"

His head flung up. He stared at her. "I—*I* wanted that? Léa. You found the TV spots. You cheered when I succeeded. You handed me your father's restaurant and expected me to save it."

"We were in it together!" she said, stunned. Him and her, shoulder to shoulder, against the world. There hadn't been really any way to distinguish what he wanted and she wanted, those first few years, or even who she was and who he was, both focused on the same goal. The restaurant's success. His success. Not letting the restaurant become the albatross around his neck, the weight he took on too young, but turning it into the tool that let him become all that he could be. She hadn't realized, until the day before, that Daniel had ever admitted to himself that the restaurant was too much for a nineteen-year-old chef-in-training to take on. But *she* had always known it. And she had so desperately wanted him to be able to fly as high as his oversized ambitions pushed him.

"I know that. I'll never forget it. I'll never forget how brave you were or how much you trusted me. Léa—when a man climbs a glass mountain, it's not usually for the damn golden apple. It's for the person he gives the apple to."

Her tears sprang out again, harder, but sparkling somehow with the beauty of what he had just said. "Daniel—"

"And I've *told* you this already, Léa. Yesterday, I told you. The day before I told you. How many different ways do you need to hear that every damned thing I do is for you? *Putain.* Even if you don't know what's wrong," he said, low and stark. "Just try to tell me what it is. Just try, Léa. I need to know."

Something snapped. She clutched fistfuls of the quilt suddenly and, when that wouldn't rip, flung herself off the bed. "How the hell should I *know*, Daniel? I can barely even *see* me. It's you, and my brother, and my sister, and the restaurant, and the numbers, and the damn personnel issues, and you, you, you. You're everything, and *you're* not even there, you're so busy being so huge, the best of the best of the best, it's like I wave to you from far away in the stands to cheer you on, hoping you'll glance up and see my little flag and know I care. Now you say you do it for me, but from where I'm sitting—I *think* you glance up. I *think* it matters, that I be there in the stands cheering. I *think* it makes a difference. But God knows...it's not about me. I don't care what you *say,* don't you think that I would know it, if ever once, in the past eleven years, there had been something really about *me*? Sometimes, Mondays, at lunch with my cousins, I can almost breathe, I can almost feel myself, no, I can almost feel as if I *have* a self—and then someone calls and needs me to solve something, or there's a consulting request for you and I need to figure out your schedule, or my brother's girlfriend dumped him, or...you just *look* at me, and I'm all gone again. I love you *so much* and you are *so big*, and I am *nothing*. Just nothing."

And she stood there, too exhausted to even slump back down on the bed, her head hanging as those silent tears gushed out and dripped wearily down her cheeks.

He just stared at her, stunned. His arm had dropped from the windowframe.

She brought her hands up to cover her face. "And I can't—I just can't—have kids on top of it right now. I can't. I think I'll drown."

His face had gone very white. He reached both hands behind him and gripped the lower part of the frame now, for support. "So you do need even less of me." His voice was stretched and twisted, like some bent, hard-worked piece of metal.

"No." No, that wasn't right. She—

"If I leave you feeling you're nothing." He dragged one hand over his face, too hard, leaving white marks on the sun-flush. "I—*nothing?* I gave all of me to you— *all of me*—and that made you feel as if you were *nothing?*"

Léa stared at him, across a small tropical room that seemed as vast as a great void. "I gave all of me to you," she said, low, muffled. She had never even realized it before. All of her. To him. To everyone else. "And I didn't even get you back for it. You were too busy."

And she had missed him so much. Tears poured down her cheeks again at the memory of all those times he had been so far away, in the kitchens while she handled business in some other part of the restaurant, on a TV set while she sat in the green room, in Paris while she helped her sister move into her new apartment in Nice. The distance that had grown until she looked back on those first few desperate years with *nostalgia*, because at least then they had seen each other sometimes, when she and her siblings pitched in every way they could, setting tables, waiting tables, on the line in the kitchen, prepping whatever needed prepped. Watching Daniel be glorious, watching him drive everyone before him, even her, though he reached out from time to time to squeeze her shoulder or the nape of her neck in apology, when he realized what a taskmaster he was being. She had never minded. She understood him, the need that drove him, and she knew they were in it together.

"Léa." His voice was strained and cautious. "I can't do *Top Chef,* and consult all over the world, and run a three-star restaurant, *and* be home more often. You have to choose."

"*I* have to choose?" She scrubbed her face, trying to get a grip. "Daniel, it's your choice. I don't want to limit you." She never wanted to do that. "Fly as high as you want to. I'm behind you." She was, she really was. She always had been, and so proud of him. This was just a little, stupid moment of collapse she was having.

His jaw was very hard. He clenched the window frame behind him. "Léa. I've never taken a single appearance, a single consulting job, that you didn't book for me. Or, if they spoke to me directly, that I didn't think, 'Oh, she'll like that, I should do it.' And send them to talk to my wife, about scheduling. In case she should ever look at my calendar and decide I was too fucking overbooked and maybe she would like to see me some weekend."

In the tight line of his jaw, in the rigid muscles in his arms clenching the windowsill, there was so much anger that the realization of it shoved straight across the room into her, like a truck collision. Léa stared at him.

The moment stretched, breakable or buildable. Like molten sugar that could be formed into anything wonderful, as long as you didn't let it chill too much and drop it, shattering everywhere. "I—when they came to me, they always said you wanted to do it," she said, pleating her hands. "So I would find a way to fit it in."

His mouth twisted, bittersweet. "Maybe I should have made my priorities clearer to you. Maybe *a day with my wife, the woman I'm doing all this for* should have been in your calendar system as one of those first-precedence entries that can't be changed. At least once a week, *putain*." He leaned his head back against the window frame, looking exhausted.

As exhausted as *she* felt. Daniel, who was indefatigable.

She found herself drawn closer to him, step by step, with the urge to stroke that tension off his face, to tell him it was all right.

He watched her come to him. His mouth twisted again. "You say I take up too much of your space, you say I leave you nothing, but here you are, ready to care for me again. That might be your problem, Léa." A dark, bitter pain in his voice. "The problem besides me. You make us think that care of yours is inexhaustible. Because it—almost—is. And nobody can get too much of it, *chérie*. Nobody is ever going to turn it down. It's up to you to not offer it sometimes, if you need some for yourself."

She reached up and traced those lines by his eyes. Daniel had started developing fine lines of tension around his eyes years ago, by his mid-twenties at least. They relaxed a little under her fingertips, his face weary, stricken. "I like taking care of you, actually," she murmured. "I always have. It makes me feel—special." Those damn tears filled her eyes again. "As long as you're there. As long as it seems to matter."

"I'm quitting *Top Chef*," he said suddenly, harshly. "I'm sorry, Léa, that's over. If we need some influx of cash at some point, you can talk them into paying me triple, and I'll come on as a special guest. I'm sorry, I just—" His head arched back, his neck muscles corded. "*Fuck.* As long as it seems to matter. When it's all that's ever mattered. This drives me insane." His hands flexed on the frame of the window again, and she saw the nails that held it to the wall shift.

"No!" she said, appalled at her own selfishness. "Don't quit for me! Daniel! I'll be fine."

The nails shifted more. He was literally going to rip the frame out. Strong chef's hands. "I'm not quitting *for you.* Have you listened to anything I've said? I'm quitting for *me.* If you want anything else for you, Léa, you're going to have to do it. Damn it, Léa. You say you can't give me any more. *I can't give you any more, either.*"

She drew a breath as if he had struck her. He winced at the sight, wrenching the frame. "*Fuck. Putain. Merde.* Léa. We could have hired a business manager years ago. You could have been drawing and painting beautiful sights all over the world for the past three or four years at least, every time we went out for a consulting job, instead of making friends with the chef's wife so you could help her learn how to run their business better. *Merde*, Léa, how much of our time do we spend up in Paris? It's an artist's paradise. Our *house* is an artist's paradise, the views are incredible, I wish to hell I could enjoy them more often. *Nobody* stopped you but you, because—" He broke off and sighed suddenly, like a long, drawn-out collapse, all the air and muscles leaving him until his fingers loosened the frame to rise to her face. "Because you just don't know how to take for yourself. Do you? Your giant of a father—you grew up cheering for the great man in your life, didn't you? From the margins of his attention. Taking care of your siblings. Bandaging wounds, patting his apprentices on the shoulder and promising them they could survive. Taking care of people. Never putting yourself first."

"*You* put me first, for a while," she said shyly. His release of anger and the gentleness that rose up in its place lured her in, making her want to curl into him and luxuriate in it. "When you met me. It was—I never felt anything like that. It was so *wonderful*." The way his eyes would grow so brilliant, watching her, so hungry and intent and sweet, too, as he leaned over her in the grass, stroking her cheek with a flower.

"Yes, and even that, you thought was partly for the restaurant, didn't you?" He dropped his head back against the frame again. "Eleven years," he said under his breath. And then, "I guess I did put myself first. It was so fucking addictive, being your hero. I have to say, you never made me feel like nothing, Léa. You've *always* made me feel like I was your whole world. To the point that if you stopped believing in me, I think I wouldn't exist." He gave a rough, despairing laugh. "You've got to admit, it's a beautiful irony, *chérie*. I gave myself up for you. You gave yourself up for me. And we're here scrabbling to find enough of each other we can hold onto."

"Maybe I'm not the only one who needs to establish boundaries," Léa said, reaching up to rest both hands carefully on his sticky, sunburned chest.

"Maybe," he said reluctantly. "I don't know if it's something I'm able to do. I told you I can't get enough of you. Of you being happy with me." His mouth twisted again. His eyes met hers, a glimpse of dark, bittersweet humor in the beautiful gray. "I acted like a drug addict who had had his supply threatened, when I came after you here, didn't I?"

She shook her head, her mouth curving at last, and the relaxing of those smile muscles made two more tears spill out over her cheeks. She shifted a hand to his cheek. "You acted like you. It just took me a while to realize you were acting like you. Like maybe we needed a chance to get to know each other better. Not better, differently. Out of our usual patterns."

"Yes," he said softly, lifting his own hand to her cheek, so that their touches exactly matched. "I had kind of forgotten that you ever wanted to do anything but the restaurant and…sit in my stands, cheering me on. I'm sorry, *chérie*. It's hard to refuse all of you, when you offer it so generously. And I sunk all of myself into this, too. It was hard to—see anything, but the work."

"Don't you like it at all?" Léa asked doubtfully. It was impossible to believe that someone could rise to the absolute pinnacle of an insanely demanding profession without having a passion for it. Damn it, his passion for it was so obvious. In his mind was it really, always, a passion for her?

"I hate *Top Chef* for days ahead of time, but I do enjoy the high afterward, when I win and you can't stop talking about this or that thing I did on it like I'm some superhero. I *hate it* when I lose. I want to hide in some hole where you can't see me for weeks. But I do love the rest. Food, and living with all my senses, and control. And I like being the biggest man in your life, bigger even than your father. I like being the best of the best. It's only lately that I've started to realize that the price I was paying for being the biggest man in your life was…you."

"Daniel. You do understand that there's never been any question of you losing me. I really, really only came here because I needed to…take some time for me. To figure out why I was so tired, what I needed to change. I never intended to not come back." Although for a while there, the time she wanted to stay away had seemed to stretch infinitely, no end in sight. A figment of her exhaustion, and he didn't need to know about it. Maybe some part of him suspected.

"Léa. I've been losing you for years. I do want more of you. I'm sorry. But it can be a *more* where you set up your paint things in the garden and utterly ignore me while I lie on a lounger nearby and dream up menu ideas for someone in Las Vegas, if you want. I just—I want to be around you. When we can relax. When I can be something other than a chef. And you can be whatever you want to be."

"Something other than a chef while you sketch out menu ideas?" she said wryly, her hand drifting up to run through his hair.

"You might have to help me with the concept of hobbies." His hands settled at her hips, pulling her in closer to him. That odd little curve to his mouth, the one that hid a profound reserve. "I wouldn't mind learning some other facets to myself." The tips of his fingers stroked up and down her bottom, very gently. "Maybe we could even find some hobbies we do together."

"I love you," she said softly.

His eyes brightened. "I've always loved hearing that twenty or thirty times a day. I might be a little greedy."

Or astonishingly insecure. He was so incredible, so much larger than life. Was his whole sense of himself really so dependent on her?

Maybe they did both need to switch gears in life, to take a deep breath, to let themselves expand outward instead of that spear-like drive forward all the time. It was so odd to think this about Daniel, who took the world on like he was its spear, but maybe they both needed to develop—a stronger sense of self.

He lowered his forehead to hers. "Let me stay here with you another week or so, Léa. Let me take this vacation with you. I can go help Moea turn his restaurant into something that will solve their guest problem, and you can learn how to paint again, and we can go scuba-diving. Sailing. Windsurfing. Lazing on a beach. All those things we've never done. And share the same bungalow. And maybe learn some other new things about what we want." His mouth curved, and his eyes held hers for a tiny, hot second.

She smiled, with a little flush. His fingers lifted to trace the color on her cheekbones.

"And then after that," he said more slowly, "if you want to stay on a little longer without me...I guess I'll handle that. Reasonably sanely. If you don't stay too long. And when we get back home..." He looked at her a moment, then drew a long, hard breath, bringing himself to some sticking point: "I want to hand over the day-to-day running of the kitchens to Marc," he said, referring to his *second.*

Léa's jaw dropped. Okay, so...wow. They really didn't know each other's wants *at all.* She could never, in a million years, have imagined Daniel accepting less than absolute, shining-star control over those kitchens. He had fought like a feral dog for it.

"He will be excellent at it—he already does handle it half the time, when I'm consulting or on shows. And if I don't let him have the official status, he'll leave me for a kitchen where he can be king soon anyway. There's only so long a chef with his talent can stand to be someone else's *second.*"

"But—but what if he doesn't do it the way you like it?"

"If I can handle consulting with chefs in their own kitchens and getting them to listen to me, I can handle that, Léa. It's still our restaurant. It still has the Laurier name on it. But Marc wants executive chef status enough to give up his evenings and weekends, and I don't want to do that anymore."

Léa stared at her husband. "Do you want to quit being a chef altogether?" she asked wonderingly.

"No, it's still m—*our* restaurant. But what I enjoy the most these days is consulting. I always like seeing the new restaurants; I like helping a younger chef build his dream, or an older one refresh his style; I like all the ideas I get from them in return." He hesitated again. "As long as you want to come. That was always my favorite part of consulting, you know, showing you all those new countries. I still remember how excited I was the first time I got invited out of country—I was going to be able to show my wife *Singapore*."

She laughed at the memory. They had been in their mid-twenties before the consulting thing started to hit. But they had been as excited as kids again at those first overseas invitations.

He rocked her hips against his, gently, coaxingly. "If we ever do decide to have kids, we might have to re-consider the travel. But in the meanwhile...it seems as if someone who needs to re-explore that old dream of being an artist might get a lot out of traveling. I do like it when you come into the kitchens with me and share your ideas, but you don't *have* to. You could learn to insist on time for yourself to paint and sketch while I'm in the kitchens."

"I really do want kids," she said suddenly. "I always did. Before." It felt incredibly less like drowning the last of herself, if he would be in the garden with her, playing with those children, too. Everything felt lighter.

"Let's talk about it more in a year or so. Once we get ourselves figured out." His mouth curved ruefully, and he rested a possessive hand on her belly. "Or sooner, if we're not more careful."

She leaned into his hand and him, her face relaxing, because all at once, an accidental pregnancy felt as if it would work out just fine, too.

Everything would work out. She felt as if she could breathe—truly breathe—for the first time in years. She took his other hand and curved it around her face to kiss his wrist. "We need to take more vacations. Can we make a pact? Twice a year. Tropical island, hiking in Nepal, biking along the coast, I don't care. But something where we stop. And just are."

"Together," he said, rubbing her hair. "Give me a little more warning if you need a week to yourself."

She shook her head, a gesture that brushed her lips back and forth against his wrist, so she kissed it again. "I can't believe you got so *worried* about that. Honestly, Daniel."

His fingers threaded through her hair, and he pulled her head back. "Can't you? If you came back from..." He paused. Léa didn't do things that took her away from him for more than a few hours. He was always the one away. "...helping your sister shop for her apartment," he finally said, lamely, "to find a message from me saying I was taking a break in Tahiti for I wasn't sure how long, and I didn't even take my phone so you could call me, are you sure you wouldn't worry?"

She might as well have swallowed a giant rock. That burst, in her stomach, into a thousand crawling ants of panic. Daniel—gone. Without explanation. Without her. She would have been huddled into a knot of fear on their bed, her stomach trying to gnaw its way out of her: *Why? What's going on? Why didn't he want me with him? Is he having some kind of breakdown? Is there, is there—is there someone else? Is he leaving me?*

"I'm sorry." Imagined fear strangled her voice. "I'm sorry. I didn't thin—Daniel, don't do that to me. I'm sorry."

"*Chérie.* You have never in your life hurt me on purpose. I wouldn't hurt you on purpose either. I won't do that to you. I know what it feels like."

Tears filled her eyes again. "I didn't mean to—"

"I know you didn't mean to hurt me, Léa. You don't have to tell me that." His voice turned darkly wry. "After all, it was nothing to do with me." The tears trembled. His thumb came up to rub one off her lashes before it could fall. "And don't cry. I'm glad you did it. If you hadn't, God knows how long we might have kept on this way. Until we were both entirely extinguished, maybe. And then it might have been too late."

"Two vacations a year," she said firmly, rubbing her tears away against his fingers. "No matter what. From now on. Even if it's only spending four days skiing."

"You're the scheduler, *chérie.* Put it in as one of those cannot-be-changed items, along with my time with my wife."

"I'm never putting another thing in your schedule before I talk to you about it. Ever."

"All right." He had the most beautiful smile, such a fine, chiseled, sensual mouth. "It will slow down everyone who wants to book me, and it means we'll always have to talk."

She smiled, leaning against him, feeling—rested, for the first time in months. Maybe years. Feeling blissfully happy. Just a little time together, to truly talk, was that all it had taken? And two hearts held out to each other, without reservation. Just as they always had been.

She rubbed her fingers over the hand she kept curled around her face, tracing down his fingers. Her thumb stroked back and forth over the bare base of his fourth finger. "Can I get you another wedding ring?

If you're not in the kitchens as much—would you wear it?"

His face just *lit*. "*Putain*, really?" He cupped her face with both hands, searching her eyes, and then kissed her, hard. "To replace the one I outgrew when I was twenty? I thought you would never ask."

***

FIN

THANK YOU!

Thanks so much for reading! I hope you enjoyed Daniel and Léa's story. You can catch another glimpse of Léa and Daniel in *The Chocolate Rose*, Gabriel and Jolie's story.

Or if you love stories that look at marriage in trouble, *Snow-Kissed* tells the story of Kurt and Kai, a couple trying to find their way back together after a separation. She thinks all is lost. But he refuses to give up on them.

Or for a taste of Paris and arrogant French chocolatiers, try the internationally bestselling Amour et Chocolat series. (Keep reading for a complete booklist.)

And don't miss Matt's story, coming Fall 2014! Sign up for my newsletter to be emailed the moment it's released: http://lauraflorand.com/newsletter

Thanks so much for reading!

All the best,

Laura Florand

***

Website: http://lauraflorand.com/
Twitter: https://twitter.com/LauraFlorand
Facebook: http://facebook.com/LauraFlorandAuthor
Newsletter: http://lauraflorand.com/newsletter

OTHER BOOKS BY LAURA FLORAND

Snow Queen Duology

Snow-Kissed (a novella)

Sun-Kissed (also part of the Amour et Chocolat series)

Amour et Chocolat Series

All's Fair in Love and Chocolate, a novella in Kiss the Bride

The Chocolate Thief

The Chocolate Kiss

The Chocolate Rose (also part of La Vie en Roses series)

The Chocolate Touch

The Chocolate Heart

The Chocolate Temptation

Sun-Kissed (also a sequel to Snow-Kissed)

La Vie en Roses Series

Turning Up the Heat (a novella)

The Chocolate Rose (also part of the Amour et Chocolat series)

A Rose in Winter, a novella in No Place Like Home

Memoir

Blame It on Paris

THE CHOCOLATE ROSE

The scent of jasmine wafted over Jolie as she stepped into the place, delicate and elusive, as the breeze stirred vines massed over sun-pale walls. A surprisingly quixotic and modern fountain rippled water softly in the center of a tranquil, shaded area of cobblestones. She stopped beneath the fountain's stylized, edgy angel, dipping her hand into the water streaming from the golden rose it held. Fontaine Delange, said a little plaque.

Gabriel had a city fountain named after him already? Well, why not? There were only twenty-six three-star restaurants in France, eighty in the world. He had put this little town on the map.

His restaurant, Aux Anges, climbed up above the place in jumbled levels of ancient stone, a restored olive mill. She would have loved to sit under one of those little white parasols on its packed terrace high above, soaking up the view and exquisite food, biding her time until the kitchens calmed down after lunch. But, of course, his tables would be booked months in advance. In another restaurant, she might have been able to trade on her father's name and her own nascent credentials as a food writer, but the name Manon was not going to do her any favors here.

The scents, the heat, the sound of the fountain, the ancient worn stone all around her, all seemed to reach straight inside her and flick her tight-wound soul, loosing it in a rush. Stop. It will be all right. Your father is out of immediate danger, has two other daughters, and will survive a day without you. Take your time, take a breath of that hot-sweet-crisp air. Relief filled her at the same time as the air in her lungs. That breath smelled nothing like hospitals, or therapists' offices, or the stubborn, heavy despair in her father's apartment that seemed as unshakeable as the grime in the Paris air.

She walked past an art gallery and another restaurant that delighted in welcoming all the naive tourists who had tried showing up at Aux Anges without reservations. A little auberge, or inn, gave onto the place, jasmine vines crawling all over its stone walls, red geraniums brightening its balconies.

She turned down another street, then another, weaving her way to a secret, narrow alley, shaded by buildings that leaned close enough for a kiss, laundry stretching between balconies. Jasmine grew everywhere, tiny white flowers brushing their rich scent across her face.

Kitchen noises would always evoke summer for her, summer and her visits to France and her father. The open windows and back door of Aux Anges let out heat, and the noises of knives and pots and people yelling, and a cacophony of scents: olive oil, lavender, nuts, meat, caramel. . . .

As she approached the open door, the yelling grew louder, the same words overheard a million times in her father's kitchens: "Service! J'ai dit service, merde, it's going to be ruined. SERVICE, S'IL VOUS PLAÎT!"

"—Fast as we can, merde – putain, watch out!"

A cascade of dishes. Outraged yells. Insults echoed against the stone.

She peeked through the door, unable to resist. As a child and teenager, she had been the kid outside a candy shop, confined to her father's office, gazing at all that action, all that life: the insane speed and control and volcanic explosions as great culinary wonders were birthed and sent forth to be eaten.

At least fifteen people in white and black blurred through a futuristic forest of steel and marble. Four people seemed to be doing the yelling, two chefs in white, two waiters in black tuxedos, separated by a wide counter and second higher shelf of steel: the pass, through which elegant plates slipped into the hands of waiters, who carried them into the dining rooms with—ideally—barely a second's pause between when the plate was finished and when it headed toward the customer who was its destination. A wave of profound nostalgia swept Jolie.

"Connard!" somebody yelled.

"C'est toi, le connard, putain!"

A big body straightened from the counter closest to the door and turned toward the scene, blocking her view of anything but those broad shoulders. Thick, overlong hair in a rich, dark brown, threaded with gold like a molten dark caramel, fell over the collar of the big man's chef's jacket, a collar marked with the bleu, blanc, rouge of a Meilleur Ouvrier de France. That bleu, blanc, rouge meant the chef could only be one person, but he certainly wasn't skinny anymore. He had filled into that space she had used to only imagine him taking up, all muscled now and absolutely sure.

His growl started low and built, built, until it filled the kitchen and spilled out into the street as a full-bodied beast's roar, until she clapped her hands to her head to hold her hair on. Her ears buzzed until she wanted to reach inside them and somehow scratch the itch of it off.

When it died down, there was dead silence. She gripped the edge of the stone wall by the door, her body tingling everywhere. Her nipples felt tight against her bra. Her skin hungered to be rubbed very hard.

Gabriel Delange turned like a lion who had just finished chastising his cubs and spotted her.

Her heart thumped as if she had been caught out on the savannah without a rifle. Her fight instinct urged her to stalk across the small space between them, sink her hands into that thick hair, jerk her body up him, and kiss that mouth of his until he stopped roaring with it.

That would teach him.

And her flight option wanted to stretch her arm a little higher on that door, exposing her vulnerable body to be savaged.

She gripped that stone so hard it scraped her palm, fighting both urges.

Gabriel stood still, gazing at her. Behind him, the frozen tableau melted: petits commis, waiters, sous-chefs, all returning to their tasks with high-speed efficiency, the dispute evaporated. Someone started cleaning up the fallen dishes. Someone else whipped a prepped plate off the wall, where little prongs allowed them to be stacked without touching each other, and began to form another magical creation on top of it.

Jo tried to remember the professional motivation of her visit. She was wearing her let's-talk-about-this-professionally pants. She was wearing her but-this-is-a-friendly-visit little sandals. Given the way her nipples were tingling, she would have preferred that her casually formal blouse have survived her one attempt to eat chocolate in the car while she was wandering around lost for hours, but no . . . her silky pale camisole was all she had left.

Gabriel's eyebrows rose just a little as his gaze flicked over her. Curious. Perhaps intrigued. Cautiously so.

"You're late," he said flatly.

"I had a lot of car trouble," she apologized. It sounded better than saying she had spent hours circling Sainte-Mère and Sainte-Mère-Centre and Sainte-Mère-Vieux-Village, utterly lost. Wait, how did he know she was late? This was a surprise visit. "I'm sorry. I know this is a bad time."

"Bon, allez." He thrust a folded bundle of white cloth at her. She recognized the sturdy texture of it instantly: a chef's jacket. A heavy professional apron followed. His gaze flicked over her again. "Where are your shoes?"

"I—"

"If you drop hot caramel on those painted toenails, I don't want to hear about it. Coming to work without your shoes. I thought Aurélie told me you had interned with Daniel Laurier."

"Uh—"

Eyes blue as the azure coast tightened at the corners. "You made it up to get a chance. Parfait. And you're late. That's all I need. Get dressed and go help Thomas with the grapefruit."

Probably she should have told him right then.

But . . . she had been having a hellish two months, and . . . a sneak peek into Gabriel Delange's kitchens. . . .

A chance to work there through a lunch hour, to pretend she was part of it all. Not in an office. Not observing a chef's careful, dumbed-down demonstration. Part of it.

She had spent the past two months dealing with hospitals and fear and grief, and he had just handed her happiness on a plate. What was an impassioned food writer to do?

Not the ethical thing, that was for darn sure.

***

Available now!

ABOUT LAURA FLORAND

Laura Florand was born in Georgia, but the travel bug bit her early. After a Fulbright year in Tahiti, a semester in Spain, and backpacking everywhere from New Zealand to Greece, she ended up living in Paris, where she met and married her own handsome Frenchman. She is now a lecturer at Duke University and very dedicated to her research into French chocolate. For some behind the scenes glimpses of that research, please visit her website and blog at http://lauraflorand.com. You can also join the conversation on Facebook at http://facebook.com/LauraFlorandAuthor or email Laura at laura@lauraflorand.com.

COPYRIGHT

Made in the USA
Charleston, SC
12 March 2015